Eden's scream

She stared at the t[...]
He aimed a gun at [...] hand
over her tummy, she asked, "wn-what do you want?"

His gun wavered, but he didn't answer. He lunged for
Eden at the same moment Zach's K-9, Amber, lunged
at the gunman.

"No!" Eden darted out of reach.

Zach tackled the intruder to the ground. The gun flew
out of the assailant's hand and slid under the couch. As
they wrestled on the carpet, Amber clenched her teeth
around the man's arm.

"Out!" Zach commanded Amber to release.

The K-9 immediately let go but stayed close, snarling
and barking. Zach grabbed the intruder, landing a hard
punch. When it seemed as if Zach was succeeding, the
attacker reared up, hitting Zach with a force that had
him falling back...

* * *

DAKOTA K-9 UNIT

Award-winning, multi-published author **Terri Reed** writes heartwarming romance and heart-pounding suspense. Her books have appeared on *Publishers Weekly* top ten, Nielsen BookScan top fifty and Amazon Bestseller lists and featured in *USA TODAY*. When not writing, she can be found doing agility with her dog or digging in her garden. You can visit her online at www.terrireed.com, sign up for her newsletter for exclusive content or email her at terrireedauthor@terrireed.com.

Books by Terri Reed

Love Inspired Suspense

Christmas Protection Detail
Secret Sabotage
Forced to Flee
Forced to Hide
Undercover Christmas Escape
Shielding the Innocent Target
Trained to Protect

Pacific Northwest K-9 Unit

Explosive Trail

Mountain Country K-9 Unit

Search and Detect

Dakota K-9 Unit

Standing Watch

Visit the Author Profile page at LoveInspired.com for more titles.

STANDING WATCH

TERRI REED

LOVE INSPIRED SUSPENSE
INSPIRATIONAL ROMANCE

Special thanks and acknowledgment are given to Terri Reed for her contribution to the Dakota K-9 Unit miniseries.

LOVE INSPIRED® SUSPENSE
INSPIRATIONAL ROMANCE

ISBN-13: 978-1-335-63874-8

Standing Watch

Recycling programs
for this product may
not exist in your area.

Love Inspired
22 Adelaide St. West, 41st Floor
Toronto, Ontario M5H 4E3, Canada
www.LoveInspired.com

Printed in Lithuania

MIX
Paper | Supporting
responsible forestry
FSC® C021394

And we know that all things work together for good
to them that love God, to them who are the called
according to his purpose.
—*Romans* 8:28

To my wonderful husband, who loves me well.

ONE

"Two hundred and ten." Interpretive Park Ranger Eden Kelcey counted each step of the Presidential Trail staircase leading to the observation deck below the iconic memorial at Mount Rushmore National Memorial, South Dakota.

The crisp early morning air cooled her face, but her uniform's light green, long-sleeved cotton shirt kept her body warm, and her flat-brimmed hat shaded her face. The June sun tipped over the tree line of ponderosa pine, aspen and spruce, chasing away the shadows of the park.

But not the shadows on her heart.

Every morning for the past six years, Eden walked her daily patrol ahead of the public, who were just now beginning to arrive, looking for any trash or graffiti that the tourists who visited the park the day before might have left behind. But today her heart wasn't fully engaged in her job.

"Three hundred," she continued to count as she forced each foot onto the next stair. The paved path wound through the park in a series of zigzagging staircases around the magnificent trees scattered over the hill, toward the outcropping of granite rock. There, visitors could pause on the terrace below the four presidents' faces chiseled into the stone mountain before moving down another set of stairs.

Fatigue pulled at her. The bouts of emotional upheaval were disturbing her sleep and upsetting her stomach. Though she hadn't had much of an appetite, her waistline seemed to be expanding. Focusing required more brain power lately. She supposed sorrow over her marriage ending was bound to wreak havoc on her system. Her husband, Zach, had moved out two months ago, and they'd had little contact since. She missed him, but it was for the best, especially after how they'd left things. The relationship was over.

Her gaze roamed back and forth along the wooded terrain on either side of the staircase, searching for anything out of place. Unfortunately, some didn't abide by the law and snuck into the park after hours or off the official trails.

The sound of voices, that of a man and a woman, raised in anger drifted on the breeze. Abandoning her counting, she hurried up the last few flights of stairs and reached the Talus Terrace observation deck to see a bushy blond-haired man wearing mirrored sunglasses, jeans and a bulky jacket arguing with one of the younger park rangers, Lindsay Nash.

The petite brunette kept to herself most of the time. Eden hadn't spent much time with Lindsay and had only a handful of conversations with her, learning she was from Pennsylvania.

Suddenly, the man lunged forward, towering over Lindsay as his hands wrapped around her throat, knocking her flat-brimmed hat eschewed. Before Eden could even blink or move, he'd pushed Lindsay back against the railing. The young ranger scratched at the man's gloved hands, her eyes rolling back as he strangled her.

A rush of adrenaline and fear coursed through Eden as she hurried forward to help Lindsay.

"Hey!" Eden shouted and grabbed for her radio on her shoulder.

The man's head turned in Eden's direction. She couldn't see his eyes behind his glasses, but the sneer on his lips gave her pause. He released Lindsay, who crumpled to the ground in a heap.

Please, God, don't let her be dead.

The thought barely formed before the man pivoted and lurched in long rapid strides toward Eden.

Self-preservation kicked in. She raced to the railing and hopped over, landing six feet down onto the dirt ground. Momentum had her falling forward, releasing her hold on the radio. She tucked and rolled. The impact reverberated through her limbs as dirt and debris bit into her flesh through the cotton of her uniform.

A thud and grunt came from the man as he landed not far away. He'd followed her over the stair railing.

Eden scrambled to her feet and ran down the hill toward the park entrance.

"Help! Someone help me!" she cried, praying that her voice would carry through the park and maybe one of the other rangers getting ready for their morning tour would hear and come to her aid.

Her hands fumbled to regrasp the radio attached to her shoulder, but it slipped from her grip and hung down her back, bouncing painfully against her spine with each step.

Behind her, the pounding footsteps of Lindsay's attacker sounded like a herd of charging buffalo. He was gaining on her, his longer stride eating up the space she was trying to put between them. She forced her legs to pump faster, harder, digging into the dirt as she zigzagged around the thick-trunked ponderosas and the spindly aspens. She jumped over small granite boulders and climbed over others in her quest to escape.

Strong arms wrapped around her waist as the man tackled her to the ground.

A scream wrenched from her body. Her head hit something hard, pain exploded, stealing her breath, and then the world blinked out.

"Did you hear that?" Keystone Sheriff's Deputy K-9 Officer Zach Kelcey halted and put a hand up to stop his colleague Plains City Police Detective West Cole.

Zach's dog, Amber, a female black Labrador retriever, named for the bright color of her eyes, stood still, her ears shifting back and forth. Specializing in search and rescue, Amber immediately went into working mode. A cry for help was the first trigger. Her snout lifted, and her nose muscles twitched as she sniffed through the scents of the forest.

"A scream," West said, bringing his K-9, a beagle named Peanut, to a halt. The two had only recently been paired after West's K-9 had died in a shoot-out. Zach had heard that the brown and white beagle had once belonged to deceased Plains City Police Detective Kenyon Graves. Peanut was specially trained to detect gunpowder and gun oil, a specialty they'd intended to use today.

As members of the recently formed Dakota Gun Task Force, Zach and West were in the national state park searching for buried weapons. Word on the street was that the trafficking ring the task force was working to bring down was using major landmarks to hide caches of illegal arms buried in metal boxes. Zach had volunteered to search Mount Rushmore because he was from nearby Keystone and knew the park well, but mostly because his wife worked here, and he wanted to make sure she was safe. He and Eden may be separated and heading toward dissolving their marriage, but he still cared.

Zach searched the sloped terrain. Trees and bushes grew in every direction except for where the granite rock of Mount Rushmore jutted out of the ground and loomed high overhead. "Before the scream... It was a cry for help. It sounded like Eden." But what were the chances that his estranged wife was actually in trouble?

It had to be his imagination conjured up by the guilt and sorrow of their separation crowding his chest.

"Eden, as in your wife?"

West's puzzled expression only ratcheted up Zach's anxiety as he took off at a run toward where the scream had come from. "She's a park ranger here. But the call for help didn't come from the paved paths she normally works but deeper in the forest." In the off-limits area. Maybe she had seen something, or someone, burying the weapons Zach and West were hunting.

His heart lurched, but he slowed enough to dig to the bottom of his rucksack and pulled out one of Eden's scarves, which he'd found in his truck and meant to give back when next he checked in with her.

He held the colorful piece of silk under Amber's nose and then gave the command, "Find."

Amber's nose twitched. She turned in a circle, her snout in the air, searching for a whiff of odor on the wind. In all his years of search and rescue, concentrating mostly on missing children, he'd never felt this sort of helplessness.

Only one other time in his life had he ever experienced this powerless, devastating emotion. The day his four-year-old sister had wandered away from the house. He'd been tasked with babysitting duty while his parents went golfing at some charity event.

Between both Mom and Dad's jobs and their social calendar, they'd kept busy.

But Zach's eleven-year-old self had been too angry at his parents for once again leaving him in charge and too consumed with playing video games to pay attention to Caron. She'd been found hours later in a nearby barn, unconscious from a kick by a horse.

His fault.

Though Caron had recovered with a limp, his life changed that day. He'd vowed then to never have children of his own that he would be ultimately responsible for. And he was paying his penance by helping to make sure no other child stayed lost.

Amber turned suddenly and sprinted forward, nearly jerking Zach off his feet. He released the leash, letting it drag behind the K-9, and charged after her. West and Peanut followed.

"Eden!" Zach called out.

Off to his right, he heard something, or someone, crashing through the thick underbrush of the forest, but Amber was headed in the opposite direction. He stayed with his dog. West and Peanut peeled off to track whatever made the noise.

Up ahead a person lay crumpled on the ground. A flat-brimmed ranger hat tipped upside down rested a few feet away. Sunlight glinted off waves of strawberry blond hair.

Eden.

Zach's stomach bottomed out. No!

Amber skidded to a halt and dropped down on her belly. The dog let out a plaintive whine.

Heart thundering in his chest, Zach reached his wife. Blood matted her hair near her temple. More blood covered a wide circle, darkening the ground and the granite rock beneath her head. She'd obviously taken a tumble. Sticks, dry needles and debris clung to her uniform. What was she doing off the paved trail?

Zach dropped to his knees. *Oh God, please don't let her be dead.*

He pressed two fingers to her carotid artery and felt the faint thud of her heartbeat. Relief was swift, but on its heels was terror. They had to stop the bleeding. He grasped her shoulder and gently jostled her. "Eden."

She didn't rouse.

West and Peanut joined him. The beagle sniffed at Eden. Amber nudged the dog aside as if to protect Eden from the smaller canine.

"I've called 911," West said. "We didn't see anyone."

Afraid to move Eden for fear that she'd broken her neck, Zach clasped her hand. The diamond wedding solitaire soldered to a gold band winked up at him making his heart clench. "Come on, Eden. Wake up. Please." His chest rose with rapid breaths, and every cell in his body tensed with the need to know she was okay.

But how could she be? His wife lay bleeding at his feet. How had she come to harm? He vowed he'd do everything in his power to find out.

Zach's voice called to Eden. Somewhere in her mind, she wanted to curl into that voice, into the dream of the husband and family she'd longed for.

But no.

He'd made it clear he didn't want children. He didn't want a family. And by extension, didn't want her or the life she'd hoped to have with him.

She'd made a mistake to assume he wanted children. He worked with kids all the time in his search and rescue job, and when they'd married she'd never imagined that he didn't want to be a dad.

A groan echoed in her ears. With a start, she realized she'd made the sound. Something wet and rough swiped across her cheek. Her hand was encased in warmth. Her eyelids fluttered open, and she winced against the June sun overhead.

Squinting, she focused as her estranged husband's face came into view. Had she conjured him up or was this real?

She turned her head to find herself nose-to-nose with Amber. The dog licked her face again. No, this was real.

Zach couldn't be here. Seeing him hurt. She didn't want to hurt anymore. Her gaze dropped to their joined hands. Both of their wedding rings reflected the bright sun.

Her heart thudded. He still wore his wedding ring.

As did she. Clearly, neither of them had accepted the bleak future laid out before them.

Eden's tongue was thick in her mouth. "Why are you here? What happened?"

"That's what I'd like to know."

The hard edge to Zach's voice shook her. Why was he angry? He was the one to hold back, to decide he didn't want a life with her. He didn't get to be angry.

Then the events of the morning came flooding back. Zach was the least of her worries. She gasped and tried to sit up. "Lindsay."

"Did she attack you?" Zach slipped an arm around her shoulders, cradling her against his chest.

Trying not to be distracted by the scent of his aftershave, the one she'd bought him for Christmas, she said, "No. She's on the Talus Terrace observation deck. You must help her. He—" A sob escaped as the horror of what that man had done swamped her. "He ran away, I think. I don't know. He tackled me. I must have hit my head."

With her free hand, she touched the wound near her temple and winced at the sting of her fingers probing the site.

"EMTs are on their way." A tall, blond-haired, blue-eyed man came into view. He wore a police officer's uniform. Not from Keystone. "Peanut and I will go to the observation deck and see if we can help Lindsay."

Eden watched as they hustled away. "Who's that?"

"A colleague," Zach answered. "You said a man tackled you. Who?" He shifted so they were face-to-face. "Who did this to you? Why?"

She stared at her ruggedly handsome husband, taking in his thick, tousled brown hair and warm brown eyes. Her heart squeezed tight with yearning, but she pushed it away. She couldn't let herself soften toward him. She had to stay resolved in what needed to be done. Ending their marriage was for the best.

Because she wanted to be a mother more than anything else.

And he didn't want children.

How could they ever reconcile the disparity? A piercing pain arrowed through her. Anger chased after. She breathed in, manufacturing a calm that kept her from lashing out at him.

Forcing herself to focus on Zach's questions, she said, "I don't know who he was or what he and Lindsay disagreed about. I don't know why she was there so early." Guilt pricked her like the pine needles beneath her. "If I'd only arrived sooner..." She shuddered and closed her eyes on the memory of seeing Lindsay falling to the ground. "He choked her."

"What did he look like?" Zach gently prodded.

Opening her eyes, Eden recalled the man to mind. "Caucasian. Blond. He towered over Lindsay, which isn't saying much since she's petite." Eden shook her head and swallowed back the bile crawling up her throat. "He wore large mirrored sunglasses. Jeans. A bulky bomber-type jacket."

"How did you end up here?" Zach made a sweeping gesture with his hand toward the rock and forest.

Remembering the maliciousness coming off the man sent a fresh shiver of fear through her. She explained all that had led up to her trying to get away from him. "I jumped over the stair railing, and he followed me."

"Could you identify him—if he took off the sunglasses and jacket?"

"I'm not sure." She tried to conjure his image clearly and failed. "I don't think so," she admitted. "It happened so fast."

"But he doesn't know that." Zach's throaty tone held a note she'd never heard from him before. "You're in danger."

His pronouncement sent a chill of dread chasing over her flesh. Would Lindsay's assailant really come after her?

TWO

When the EMTs arrived, Zach stepped back, allowing the two paramedics to assess Eden. She'd taken a blow to the head and passed out. That was never a good thing. A black bird swooped past, drawing his gaze.

His heart thudded too fast and sweat broke out along his brow. Eden could have died. The thought made his blood turn cold. And whether she could identify her attacker or not, the attacker could identify her. Would the assailant come after her?

A flinch of dread spasmed within his gut.

Zach needed to get to the bottom of what happened. Eden was supposed to be safe in the park.

He knew better than to allow his heart to ever attach to anyone. After nearly losing his sister because of his selfishness, he'd decided never to be vulnerable to heartache. A decision that had cost him many relationships over the years.

Until he'd met Eden.

He'd fallen for her hard and fast, against his better judgment.

His dad had warned him that he was being rash in asking Eden to marry him only two months after their first date. For once, Zach hadn't listened. Now he was paying the price. They both were. She was going to divorce him. Or was she? She still wore his wedding ring. Regret as sharp as a tactical knife slashed through him. She deserved the life she wanted. The life she'd earned.

The life he couldn't give to her. He just couldn't. But he would do everything in his power to keep her safe.

West and Peanut returned. The beagle flopped down on his haunches and panted. West's grim expression didn't bode well. Gesturing with his head, West indicated he needed to speak to Zach out of earshot of Eden and the paramedics.

Reluctant to leave Eden's side, Zach had Amber stay with Eden. The big black Lab glanced at Zach in acknowledgment, then returned her attention to Eden.

Zach walked a few feet away but stood where he could keep an eye on Eden. He rolled his shoulder, relieving some of the residual pain from having it dislocated last month. "What did you find?"

"There's a dead woman on the observation deck," West told him. "A park ranger. Strangled. Though I think her neck might actually be broken. Your fellow Pennington County deputies are on the scene. The county coroner is on the way."

Alarm took hold of Zach. A tremor ripped through him. "Eden saw the killer."

West glanced over to where Eden sat. "What has she said?"

"Lindsay and a blond man were arguing. He attacked Lindsay then came after Eden when she tried to intervene."

"He might try again," West said, coming to the same conclusion Zach had just moments before.

"Yes. But he'll have to go through me to get to her," Zach vowed.

West nodded, then gave him a look rife with meaning. "She'll need to give a statement to someone other than her husband."

As a deputy sheriff and a sworn federal officer of the task force, Zach was more than qualified to record her statement, but he did understand that it would be less problematic if she talked to another deputy. "She will."

"We're going to take her to the hospital," one of the paramedics called out.

Zach and West, with Peanut close, returned to Eden's side.

"We should put you on a backboard to take you out of the park," the other paramedic told Eden.

"I don't need to be carried." Eden moved to stand. "I can walk."

"Ma'am, it's protocol," the paramedic insisted.

Zach hustled forward, taking her arm and helping her to her feet. Amber moved in on her other side as if to help. "You should listen to the paramedics."

She swayed, then her knees buckled.

Stubborn woman. Zach scooped her up into his arms. "I'll carry you out."

After a brief hesitation, she threaded her arms around his neck and laid her head on his chest. "You don't have to do this."

"Yes, I do," Zach said. "And you're going to the hospital."

"Nothing a bandage and a day of rest won't cure," she griped.

"You heard the paramedics. Unconsciousness. Lots of blood loss."

Her eyelids fluttered closed. "You're bossy."

"You're just now figuring that out?" He shook his head. They really didn't know each other very well. Yes, they'd been married for a year, but between his job and her job, they really hadn't spent a lot of time together.

And now that he'd joined the task force, there would be even less time.

No, that wasn't true. He'd make the time to see to her safety because at the end of the day he loved her. He just couldn't give her what she wanted. He didn't want to be the one to stand in the way of her dream.

* * *

With Zach carrying her to the park's entrance and the paramedics following closely behind, Eden wanted to rewind time and start the day over.

If she hadn't been so distracted by her own pain and sorrow, she might have reached the observation platform in time to save Lindsay.

But if she had the power to rewind time she'd also go back to that summer day when she'd met Zach.

If for no other reason than to ask him if he wanted children and to build a family. Had she known up front that he didn't, she might have reconsidered marrying him no matter how much she loved him. She knew there was no guarantee they could have children, but at least they would have had a shared dream. A dream she still held dear. But now her trust in him was in tatters. They'd been apart for too long to make their marriage work.

There was no rewinding time. She had to face reality.

Lindsay was dead. Eden had heard West tell Zach as much, even though he'd tried to keep his voice low. A fresh wave of grief washed over Eden. That poor young woman. Her poor family. They would be devastated.

Zach's long legs ate up the ground as he made his way toward the entrance to the park. She noted the park's visitors on the Avenue of Flags staring at them. She searched the many faces for the man who'd strangled Lindsay but didn't see anyone with bushy blond hair and mirrored sunglasses.

Zach carried her out of the park's entrance pergola to the waiting ambulance. The two paramedics rushed past to open the back bay doors. One paramedic slid a wheel gurney out and prepared it for her. Zach gently set her down on the portable bed. She stretched out her legs and leaned into the pillowed backrest. The throbbing in her head intensified. The rock she'd smacked against had really done a number on her.

A group of fellow park rangers had gathered nearby. One man broke away and headed toward them. Her boss, Matt Acosta. In his late forties, married with three children, the man was a surrogate father to the younger summer help. Eden, at nearly thirty, had always admired Matt and his wife, Amy, and their commitment to family. Matt had once been an army ranger before moving to Keystone and working his way up through the National Park Service. A trajectory Eden wanted to emulate.

"Please, tell me you're okay," Matt said as he joined Eden and Zach at the back bay of the ambulance. His dark eyes were filled with concern.

"I'm okay," she told him. "I took a nasty fall."

"No fall. You were pushed," Zach stated in a harsh tone.

She winced but refrained from glancing at Zach. She'd never seen this side of him. She wasn't afraid of him but more curious as to why he was reacting so insensitively to her situation. Was he still angry and hurt from their last conversation? They'd both said unkind things, made accusations, and had parted on a negative note.

"I heard there was a fatality. Lindsay Nash? She's not on the schedule for today," Matt said.

Tears gathered in Eden's eyes. "She was so young."

Matt's gaze went to the monument of the presidents. "Why would somebody kill one of our rangers? Why would someone want to kill Lindsay?"

Another man joined them. "That's what I intend to find out."

Zach turned to the newcomer and held out his hand. "Sam, it's good to see you."

Eden was also glad to see Sam Powell of the Pennington County Sheriff's Investigation Division. He was a friend of Zach's and by extension a friend of hers. At least she hoped. Though once her and Zach's marriage was officially over, would the new circle of friends she'd enjoyed for the past year stick around? Or would they all abandon her? Her heart weighed heavy in her chest.

Maybe she should've prayed that God would

change the desires of her heart rather than clinging to her dreams of children and family.

Exhaustion tugged at the edges of her mind,
forcing her to push away thoughts of the future.
She closed her eyes, needing a moment to rest.
But her blood thrummed too fast, and her pulse
beat in her throat. Images of the man's hands
around Lindsay's neck tormented Eden.

The paramedics lifted the gurney. She jolted
and blinked back the grogginess wanting to claim
her. Once she was settled into the bay of the ambulance, her gaze took in all of her colleagues,
her estranged husband and her boss staring at
her. A flush of embarrassment had her face flam-
ing. Some people thrived in the spotlight, but she
didn't like being the center of attention. Especially not when she was on the brink of losing
consciousness.

Amber whined. Zach looked to the paramedic.
"Can we join you? She's my wife."

Eden's pulse spiked. His wife. Not for much
longer. Guilt and disappointment flooded her
veins.

The paramedic's eyebrows shot up. "If it's okay
with her."

Eden met Zach's gaze. She wanted to say no.
She wanted him to honor the separation that
they'd agreed to. But she didn't have the where-
withal to refuse him. And deep down inside she
knew she didn't want to. She felt safe and pro-

tected when he was near. Always had. And apparently, always would.

Despite this weakness that would one day come back to haunt her, she nodded her agreement for him to join her in the ambulance bay. Her gaze bounced to Amber, meeting the K-9's trusting eyes. She loved the dog and needed the comfort of the pretty Labrador.

Zach climbed in and settled Amber between his feet. Once the vehicle was moving, taking them out of the park and onto the highway, he said, "I'll call your dad."

"He's in Alaska fishing. I don't want to interrupt his vacation."

The censuring look Zach gave her twisted her tummy into a pretzel. Her father would come back straightaway when he learned of the attack. But it would take several days for him to leave the wilds of Alaska and fly home. However, she would feel safe with him there, and Zach could be released from taking care of her. "I'll call him tonight."

Zach reached for Eden's hand, but she quickly tucked her hands beneath the blanket the paramedic put over her. Tremors worked through her body. Logically, she knew it was shock and the adrenaline letdown from witnessing Lindsay Nash's murder. Not to mention being chased by the killer, pushed downhill and left for dead had her crashing emotionally as well as physically.

Amber maneuvered her thick torso around to

face the doors. The Labrador's tail stood straight up, and her ears jutted back as she stared out the ambulance bay rectangular windows. She let out a series of barks that reverberated through the space and made Eden wince.

Zach sat forward, following his dog's gaze out the windows in the rear doors. "What's this truck doing?"

Eden sat up on her elbows to see what was happening. Anxiety gripped her chest. A large black 4x4 truck rode the back bumper of the ambulance. Sunlight glinted off the driver's mirrored sunglasses.

She gasped. Fear resurged, tightening her gut. The killer clearly intended to finish the job of silencing the lone witness to his crime of murder. "It's him."

The black truck banged into the bumper, causing the ambulance to fishtail. But the driver kept control of the heavy vehicle.

Eden was knocked back to the pillow. She clung to the railings of the gurney. The paramedic grabbed for the sides of his bench seat to keep from pitching forward.

Sitting next to the paramedic, Zach planted his feet wide to stabilize himself, held on to Amber with one powerful hand and grabbed his radio with the other. His voice held an urgent tone as he called for backup.

Within moments, the distant distinct sound

of a police siren mingled with the ambulance's siren, creating a cacophony of noise that assaulted Eden's ears. The truck veered sharply into the oncoming traffic and sped past the ambulance, out of Eden's sight.

Zach moved to see out the front window. He relayed the truck's license plate to the dispatcher on the radio. Then he went back to his seat and put his hand on her shoulder. "He's gone."

Breathing deeply, she nodded and grabbed his hand. He threaded his fingers through hers. For the time being, she allowed herself to cling to him.

At the hospital, she was whisked into the emergency room, and Zach was held back by the hospital staff.

Sudden panic filled her. What if the murderer came after her in the hospital? "Please, let my husband in here. He's a sheriff's deputy."

The head nurse, a stout woman with a beautiful smile, said, "Of course, we'll let him in, honey."

A few minutes later, Zach and Amber joined her. The dog got many censuring looks from the staff and other patients, but Eden only cared that Zach and Amber were by her side. Not only because he and his K-9 could protect her, but because Zach was the one she reached for when she had a nightmare. The one she turned to for comfort when sad or hurt. It killed her to admit she was glad he was there.

Zach's words that she was in danger echoed through her mind, filling every space with a deep sense of dread. When would the killer try to get to her next? Would he try here in the hospital? Or at home? On the job next time she was in the park? When she was alone at night? What kind of future would she have now that she and the man she'd pledged her heart to were separated with no way of reconciling?

Panic revved in her blood, making her body shake. Her breaths came in short bursts. Lights danced before her eyes. Then someone secured an oxygen mask over her nose and mouth.

"Breathe in, breathe out," the nurse said. "Just breathe. You're safe here."

Zach came into view with heartbreaking alarm on his face. Her heart stuttered. Standing at the foot of the bed, he put his hand on her shin, anchoring her to the moment. Amber lifted onto her hind legs and put her front paws on the edge of her bed and gently flexed her claws as if she wanted to help keep her from spiraling.

Over the course of the next hour, the doctor came in while the nurse took blood and hooked Eden up to an IV drip as well as a heart monitor. And she did like the nurse ordered. Breathing in, breathing out. The rhythmic motion calmed the turmoil inside. Finally, the doctor returned. "Eden, you had quite a scare today," he said. "But

I just wanted to let you both know that the baby is doing fine."

Lungs seizing, Eden blinked and tilted her head. Baby? Was she hallucinating? She must've hit her head harder than she'd first thought. She couldn't be pregnant. In the weeks leading up to their separation, they certainly hadn't been trying.

"I'm sorry, Doctor." Zach's voice was higher than normal. "What did you say?"

The doctor's gaze bounced between them. "Oh. I take it you didn't know."

Eden reached up for the oxygen mask and tore it from her face. She barely managed to force words past the lump forming in her throat. "Know what?"

"You're pregnant," the doctor said with a smile. "I would say nine weeks along, judging by the HCG levels in your blood."

Eden shook her head as the world tilted and spun. Pain exploded behind her eyes. "That's not possible. I've been careful." Her gaze jumped to Zach's. "We've been careful."

The shock she felt registered in his gaze. Then he frowned. "How could this happen?"

"I hate to be the one to break it to you," the doctor said. "But short of abstinence, no birth control is one hundred percent guaranteed."

Her breathing escalated. Zach reached over to take the oxygen mask from her hand and placed it over her nose and mouth. "Breathe. In and out."

She held his gaze, letting the ramifications of the circumstances sink in through the shock and the denial. She was pregnant. Giddy happiness bubbled up but was quickly smothered by fear, anger and dread.

She was going to be a parent with a man who didn't want to be a father.

THREE

Zach had only experienced abject terror once before. But today he'd felt it three times in the space of a few hours. First, finding his wife unconscious at the Mount Rushmore National Memorial, the second time when the big black truck tried to ram the ambulance, and now as the doctor's words echoed in his ears.

He was going to be a parent.

A father.

His stomach knotted and his chest squeezed tight.

In all the scenarios of his life, he'd never imagined this happening. Not even after Eden had begged him to give her a timeline of when he would be ready to start a family. He hadn't been able to picture himself being a father. Hadn't he already proven to be horrible at parenting when his sister had disappeared on his watch? The terror he'd felt at realizing he'd lost his baby sister lived in his bones to this day. With every missing child he searched for, he relived those traumatizing hours of not knowing if Caron was alive or if someone had abducted her. The guilt wormed through him even now.

He took the advice given to Eden. Breathing in and breathing out. The edges of his consciousness darkened. In and out. He breathed through the visceral response of his blood freezing with foreboding and his stomach churning with doubts. How could this be happening?

The doctor was saying something. Zach forced himself to concentrate on the words.

"For the next two days, I want you to rest. You have a mild concussion," the doctor was telling Eden. "On your way home, I would suggest you stop at the pharmacy and get some prenatal vitamins. And I'll write you a referral to an ob-gyn."

"She's being released?" Zach asked as he sorted through the variables of taking Eden home. The need to protect her, and their baby, had his mind racing and his heart thumping. They would need to tell her father sooner than tonight, and his parents. His sister. Dread flooded his veins.

Eden had already informed her father about the separation. When Zach had told his family that his marriage was ending, his mother had clucked her disapproval, while his father had claimed not to be surprised—saying he'd known it would be only a matter of time before Zach messed up again. A clear jab at him for the incident with

Caron. And Caron, his sweet sister, had told him he was making a big mistake.

Maybe. But how could he not let Eden go?

"Yes, I will sign off on her release," the doctor said with a smile. "It'll take a few minutes for the paperwork to get processed. Congratulations to you both." The doctor turned away and pushed aside the curtain. The nurse followed, pulling the curtain shut behind them.

Zach stared at the blue polka-dotted fabric hanging from a circular rod by shiny rings, putting off the inevitable of facing his wife.

"Zach," Eden's soft voice called to him.

Hoping the distress clogging his veins didn't show in his expression he turned to her. "We'll figure this out."

There was disappointment in her eyes, but she nodded.

"Knock, knock," a masculine voice said from outside the curtain.

West. "Come in," Zach said.

West and Peanut joined them in the enclosed space. Amber lifted her head to inspect the newcomers, then settled with her snout resting on her crossed paws where she'd taken a spot on the floor.

"We found the black truck abandoned on the highway," West said. "It had been stolen out of the memorial parking lot."

Zach wasn't surprised. "Prints?"

"Wiped clean."

West turned to Eden. "We haven't been formally introduced. I'm West Cole."

Eden tugged the oxygen mask off her face. "Zach says you're on the task force with him."

"That's correct, ma'am," West said.

Zach made a face just as Eden cocked her eyebrow. "Ma'am?"

West had the good graces to appear embarrassed. "Sorry. Force of habit."

"My name is Eden," she said with a soft smile.

West smiled back. "We sure appreciate having Zach and Amber on our task force."

The nurse entered, handing Zach some paperwork and the bag with Eden's park ranger uniform and Eden a set of scrubs. "You might want to wear these."

Eden smiled her appreciation and allowed the nurse to take the oxygen mask away. "I appreciate that. I can't wait to get home and clean up."

Since Zach had ridden with West to the park, he looked at his colleague.

"I can drive you both," West said.

"You're a lifesaver," Zach said. "We'll need to stop at a pharmacy."

"There's one in the lobby of the hospital," the nurse said. "You can pick up the prenatal vitamins there."

West arched an eyebrow but didn't comment,

much to Zach's relief. He'd have to explain to his colleague later.

"Perfect. Then we can head home." He could feel Eden's gaze, so he turned to her. "Amber misses Taylor."

The corners of Eden's eyes crinkled with her smile. She knew exactly what he was doing, and he wasn't sorry for using the excuse of Amber and Eden's orange tabby cat as a reason why he was coming home with her. But the reason was so much more than that. It was his job to protect his wife and his baby.

Baby. The word alone had the power to rock him back on his heels. Combined with the fact there was a killer out there and he was after Eden, there was no way he was leaving her on her own.

"I'm sure it will be a happy reunion," Eden said. "Even if it's only for a short time."

She was laying down a boundary, letting him know she expected his visit to the house to be quick. Their house. The killer knew what she looked like. He could easily go to the park's website and find her name. And with some searching on the internet, he could find out where she lived. Nothing was private in the age of technology.

The process of discharging Eden from the hospital went smoothly. The detour to the pharmacy took little time, and soon they were tucked into West's Plains City PD SUV. The dogs had to share the compartment especially equipped for the canines, but they seemed okay with each other. Peanut was a sweetheart. Zach's heart hurt for the loss of a man he'd never met. K-9 Detective Kenyon Graves had died in an explosion while investigating the same weapons trafficking ring that the task force was charged with bringing down.

With Eden sitting in the middle between Zach and West, he had to admit to himself how good it felt to know that he was returning home. He didn't relish the storm that was coming when he revealed to Eden he was sticking around and not leaving anytime soon. But that was something they would have to discuss in private.

West pulled into the driveway of the house Zach and Eden once shared. Though it had only been two months since he left, time had a funny way of messing up his perspective. It felt like a lifetime since he'd moved into the rental house in downtown Keystone. This little bungalow on a tree-lined street outside of the city limits appeared idyllic and safe. A perfect place to raise a family. Why had he never noticed?

Flowers bloomed in Eden's garden along the walkway leading to the front porch. Amber pulled at her leash, recognizing where they were. West parked at the curb. He and his K9 followed behind them.

Before Zach could even open the front door, they heard the loud meow of Taylor, Eden's orange tabby cat.

"Okay, okay," Zach said to Amber who reacted by charging for the door. "Hold your horses." He quickly released the latch from the lead to the collar and pushed the door open.

Amber scrambled inside. Immediately, Taylor jumped at Amber and the two rolled together, then Amber jumped to her feet and bowed with her hind end in the air and her front paws stretched out. Playtime.

"Some things never change," Eden said as she stepped into the house behind Zach and took a step forward. "They need to go out back."

"Wait." Zach put his hand on her shoulder and met his colleague's gaze, silently acknowledging his need to clear the house of possible threats before allowing Eden to fully come inside. "I'll let them out. You wait here."

Using the excuse of letting the animals out in the backyard, Zach walked away. In the kitchen, he opened the slider. Amber and Taylor zoomed out into the large backyard while Peanut stayed with West.

Though he knew Amber would have alerted if there was any threat in the house, he still felt compelled to reassure himself. Making his way through the other door of the kitchen to the hallway leading to the bedrooms, Zach checked the office space and the spare bedroom, noting that many of his items had been boxed and stacked in the corner. He sucked in a painful breath, hating how things had transpired between him and Eden.

That last night two months ago, before he'd left, he'd told Eden in plain words that he had no interest in having a family, and she'd ended up in tears, saying she couldn't stay married to a man who didn't want children with her. They'd been at an impasse, where the only logical, practical thing for him to do was leave.

But life had a way of changing with unexpected events. The enormity of what they faced threatened to overwhelm him. He reminded himself to concentrate on the task at hand. Protecting Eden—and their baby—and finding a killer.

He cleared the rest of the house before returning to the living room. "All clear."

"Does that mean I can go clean up now?" Eden asked.

"Have at it." Zach made a sweeping gesture with his hand toward the primary suite at the end of the hall.

"I'm going to check in with Lucy," West said, referring to another colleague on the task force. Lucy Lopez, a K-9 officer out of Fargo, North Dakota, and her bomb detection dog, an English springer spaniel named Piper, were heading to Keystone to help with interviewing the family and friends of a dead weapons trafficker, Jared Olin, who was from the area. "She should be arriving at her hotel anytime now."

He'd had almost forgotten that she was coming. "Thank you, I appreciate it. Have her give me a call so we can discuss next steps." West would return to Plains City, where the task force was headquartered.

Once West and Peanut retreated to their vehicle, Zach stood on the porch and watched them drive away. His gaze swept the neighborhood, looking for signs of anything out of place. But everything seemed ordinary. Normal.

Zach went inside and shut the door, locking the deadbolt behind him. He headed to the backyard while Eden cleaned up.

Standing on the deck, he watched the dog and cat chase each other around the yard. He grimaced. The grass needed to be mowed. He sat on an Adirondack chair, the release of adrenalin leaving him weary. He steepled his fingers over his utility belt and sent up a prayer that God would give him strength and wisdom because right now he had no idea what he was doing or what the future would hold.

The ringing coming from his jacket pocket pulled Zach out of his thoughts of the future as a parent. The shock of learning his soon-to-be ex-wife was pregnant with his child still buzzed in his system as he watched Amber and Taylor. He glanced at the caller ID on his phone. The task force leader, ATF Supervisory Special Agent

Daniel Slater. Zach hit the talk button. "Good evening, Daniel. Sorry, I haven't checked in."

"I just got off the phone with West. He told me what happened." Daniel's voice held concern. "Is your wife okay? Are you okay?"

Appreciating Daniel's concern, Zach replied honestly, "Yes, and yes, sort of. The killer tried twice to eliminate Eden. I know I'm scheduled to do these interviews tomorrow, but I can't leave Eden alone."

"Lucy's there. She's got this. She can take point on interviews," Daniel said. "Any resources you need to help protect Eden are at your disposal. We're here for you."

Though feeling guilty for not being able to do his job at the moment, Zach needed to stay with Eden. She had to take priority. "I appreciate the offer. Once Eden's father returns from his fishing trip then I'll be more available. Mr. Schaffer used to be the sheriff before he retired."

"Sounds like he'd be a good man to have on your side," Daniel said.

"Yes. However, I'm sure I'm not his favorite person at the moment," Zach said. "But he dotes on his daughter."

"You want to explain what's going on between you and your father-in-law?"

Not really, but the fact that his year-long marriage was ending would become public knowledge soon enough. Better to give his boss a heads-up now than later. "Eden and I have been separated for the past two months."

There was a moment of silence on the other end of the phone before Daniel said, "Are you sure you want to be the one protecting Eden?"

"Yes, sir. She's still my wife and is carrying my child," Zach said. "We found out we're having a baby."

"I'd say congratulations, but I sense there's hesitation on your part."

"It's been a shock," Zach said. One he hadn't been prepared for. He didn't like being unprepared.

A beat of silence stretched. "I know your history," Daniel said. "Don't let the past color your future."

If only it was that simple.

When Daniel had brought Zach on to the task force, he'd drilled down into Zach, wanting to know what made him choose search and rescue as a focus and why missing children. Confiding the truth about how he'd let his sister and family down to his boss had been excoriating. He'd confessed that the shock and guilt of that day was what drove him to devote his career to making sure other missing children were found and brought home safely.

As a kid, he'd been awed by the search and rescue team that had discovered his sister and returned her to their family. He could still remember the team leader's words to him.

Bad things happen to everyone at some point. From here on, make sure you're part of the solution and not the problem.

Zach had taken those words to heart. His inattentiveness and irresponsibility had nearly cost his sister her life. He vowed never to be the problem again.

Outside of the family and the responding police officers, no one else knew what had happened that day with his sister. Not even Eden.

He couldn't look too deeply at why he hadn't shared this painful event with her. He was afraid to see her disappointment. The same disappointment he'd seen on his parents' faces and at times still did. They would forever blame him for his sister's injury.

Zach promised to keep his boss up-to-date on the developments of Eden's case and hung up. His next call was to Pennington County Sheriff's Deputy Sam Powell.

"Zach, I was going to ring you," Sam said by way of greeting.

"I wanted to let you know we're at the house," Zach said. "Though, I had expected to see you at the hospital."

"I stuck around the park, taking statements and making sure the body was transported to the medical examiner in Plains City."

Zach rubbed his free hand over his jaw. That could have been Eden. A shudder raced along his flesh. "Have there been any updates you can share?"

"I'd like to come over and talk to Eden," Sam said, ignoring Zach's question. "Would this evening be okay?"

"Yes, I think so. Eden needs to rest but she needs to give her statement, and I'm sure she'd like to get it over with quickly as possible," Zach said.

"Great, see you shortly." Sam hung up.

Anticipation revved through Zach's veins. With Sam's help, Zach would bring to justice the man threatening Eden and their baby.

Eden, dressed in soft velour lounge pants and a lightweight sweater for the cool June evening, hung up the phone from talking to her father. He was understandably upset that she'd been hurt but also relieved to know Zach was in the house. She'd expected him to still be angry at Zach for moving out. She'd told her dad about the trouble in their relationship when it became apparent that her marriage was ending. Dad had been sympathetic but mad at Zach.

For some reason, Eden hadn't mentioned the baby to her father. There was no logical explanation as to why she held the information back.

Maybe to spare him the additional upset? Or herself? Ugh.

She hesitated to leave her bedroom. The room she had shared with Zach. She closed her eyes against the wave of sadness. She should be resting, but she was still too freaked out by the day's events and the shocking news of her pregnancy. She and Zach needed to talk. There was so much to discuss.

Squaring her shoulders, she decided she would not settle for anything less than him being all in. If he couldn't embrace being a parent, being a father, then she needed to proceed with the separation and eventually a divorce. She would raise this child on her own and would make sure her baby never questioned her love for her or him.

With that thought firmly in place, she headed down the hall into the living room. Zach, Amber and Taylor were not there. Through the open slider to the backyard, she spied Zach sitting in an Adirondack chair. She headed out, and he was quick to stand and brought a chair over, placing it next to him.

She sat and then immediately stood. Nervous energy had her pacing the deck. "We need to talk."

"Yes," Zach said, in a wary tone. "But we have time to worry about the baby and impending parenthood."

She marveled at how he was able to know what she was referring to so easily.

"Right now," he said, "we must prepare for you to give your statement to Sam. He's on his way here."

The thought of reliving what she'd gone through today sent ribbons of anxiety winding through her. Her legs turned to rubber, and she quickly sat in the Adirondack chair next to Zach's. "I don't know what I can tell him that I haven't already told you."

"He may have additional questions that I hadn't thought of," Zach said. "I wasn't exactly being a professional today. My only concern was your safety. Your well-being."

As much as his words warmed her, a chill skated across her flesh. A man had tried to kill her today. And had succeeded in killing Lindsay. "Zach, I'm scared." She shouldn't allow herself to be vulnerable around him, yet she missed leaning on her capable husband.

Eden inhaled the crisp summer air, filled with the scents of pine and the array of blossoms growing in the flower beds lining the fence that backed up to the neighbors. Normally, she found solace in God's handiwork, but now terror consumed her. Would she ever feel safe again?

FOUR

"I'm here. I won't let anyone hurt you."

Zach reached across from his chair and took her hand. His palm was warm and comforting. Eden turned to meet his gaze. Guilt flashed in his brown eyes, and he looked away. He had hurt her. And continued to do so by not being excited by the fact they were having a child. By not wanting to make a family with her. He said they had time to talk about the baby and parenthood, but she had a sense he was deflecting, putting off something he wasn't happy about.

Extracting her hand, she mentally put up a wall between them. His lack of joy didn't matter. She would have this child on her own. With faith in God above, she would be enough. The fear sliding along her limbs mocked her resolve.

Amber raced onto the deck, her dark coat shiny in the late afternoon sunlight. She skidded to a halt in front of Zach. She sat, and her tail, thick at the base and tapering to a point, thumped against the wood. Her amber-colored eyes bore into her handler while her tongue lolled out the side of her mouth.

"Dinnertime," Zach said with a laugh.

Taylor followed Amber, winding through the dog's legs before jumping onto Eden's lap. The orange cat let out a loud meow.

Eden laughed and cuddled the feline. "I think they both are telling us they are hungry."

"They missed each other," Zach commented.

"Yes, they did," Eden agreed.

When Eden and Zach first started dating, he'd brought the dog over. Taylor, then a year old, had hidden from the Lab, but Amber was patient, not pushing for the tabby cat to play. Eventually, when Zach and Eden moved in together after their wedding, Taylor warmed up to Amber and the two became best buddies and playmates.

Zach faced her with more intensity in his eyes than she'd ever seen. "I missed you, too."

His words were like a well-placed knife. A fresh stab of hurt and anger had Eden jumping up from the chair with Taylor in her arms. For a moment the world swam with unshed tears. The edges of her vision darkened, making it clear she shouldn't move so quickly. She widened her stance and waited for the world to rebalance itself.

Zach stood, his hand coming to her elbow. "Are you okay?"

Shrugging off his concern and his hand, she

set Taylor down, turned and headed back inside. "I still have dog food in the garage."

Going through the mundane task of filling the extra dog bowl she'd kept for Amber with a scoop of kibble from the bag on the garage shelf prevented the burn of tears from fully forming. In the kitchen, she opened a can of soft cat food and dumped it into Taylor's bowl. The dog and cat ate side by side.

"Eden, I'm so sorry," Zach said from behind her, stopping short of touching her.

The heat of his body enveloped her, making her insides quiver. She closed her eyes as a fresh wave of heartache crashed into her. Everything in her wanted to relent, to curl into his embrace, but there was too much unresolved for that to happen.

A loud knock at the front door saved her from having to respond. What could she say, anyway? She couldn't absolve him for hurting her. It wasn't all right. Nothing would be right again.

Zach let Sam into the house. Eden filled a pitcher with ice water and put three glasses on a tray. She carried the tray and pitcher to the dining room table. As soon as she set the tray down, Zach grabbed the pitcher and filled the glasses. Taking a seat, she rested her elbows on the smooth wooden top and steepled her fingers. Zach set a glass of water in front of her. The ice inside the glass created beads of condensation on the outside.

"Eden, I just have a few questions for you," Sam said as he took out a notebook and pen.

Eden lifted her gaze to him. "If I can answer them, I will."

"Can you walk me through what happened to you?"

Eden frowned.

Sam's gaze was sharp. "Memory is a funny thing. It can be very malleable. You might remember something you didn't think of in the heat of the moment. Things can come back to you that didn't seem important at the time."

Bracing herself, Eden started at the beginning with her arriving at the park, clocking in and making her way down the Avenue of Flags to the Presidential Trail. She'd arrived before the park was open so there were no tourists yet. But she knew any minute they would be coming in behind her.

"I walk this path every morning, keeping an eye out for something that might've been missed the night before. We want to keep our park clean and—" Her throat clogged, choking off the word *safe*. She swallowed back the tears rising to the surface. Zach put his hands on her shoulders. The weight tethering her to the moment. "I don't know how Lindsay and this man got ahead of me."

Sam nodded. "Take your time."

Composing herself, she took a breath and exhaled before continuing. "I was near the top of the stairs when I heard arguing. I hurried up the last few flights in time to see Lindsay dressed for the day in her park ranger uniform. A large blond-haired man was towering over her."

"How much taller would you say he was than Lindsay?" Sam asked.

"She barely reached his shoulder," Eden said. The image was clear in her mind. "Lindsay had to tilt her head back to see him while wearing her flat-brimmed hat."

Sam wrote that down in his notebook. "Then what happened?"

"I was about to turn away, thinking their encounter was something private, when the man lunged at Lindsay—"

Sam held up his hand. "He lunged at her. How far away was he from her?"

Eden frowned. She closed her eyes visualizing the scene. "No more than arm's length. Maybe lunge isn't the right word. More like he pounced."

Sam continued to write in his notebook. "Then?"

"I yelled, 'Hey.'" Eden looked up at Zach and then back to Sam. "I wanted to help her. He was choking her."

Zach crouched down beside her chair. "We know you did."

"What did the man do when you yelled?" Sam prompted.

Eden swallowed. "He turned toward me."

"You saw his face?" Zach asked.

"Sort of," she said. "He had large, mirrored aviator sunglasses on."

"But you could see his jaw, his cheeks?" Sam asked. "Did he have any scars? Moles? Anything that could identify the suspect?"

Eden thought back to that moment. Her heart rate picked up. "His jaw was square."

"And his mouth? Teeth?" Sam questioned. "Did he say anything?"

"He snarled at me." Eden blinked at the memory. "He didn't say anything. Just snarled. He had big teeth." She shook her head. "I don't know. It's all so fuzzy. I mean, I only saw his face for a split second before he released Lindsay and came after me."

"You're doing great," Zach encouraged her.

"Yes, you are," Sam affirmed. "From what Zach told me, you jumped over the railing?"

"I did," Eden said. "Then I ran down the hill. I thought it would be faster than trying to take the stairs."

"When he caught up to you, did he say anything?" Sam asked.

"I don't think so. I could hear the thundering of his feet behind me then he tackled me. I hit my head and blacked out."

"Okay, I know this is difficult for you, but you're doing a perfect job. What was Lindsay doing in the park this morning? She wasn't on the schedule according to your boss," Sam said. "Could she have been filling in for someone else?"

"I suppose so. Sometimes people swap shifts," Eden said. "But we're supposed to notify HR."

"Could the man have been another park ranger?" Zach asked.

Eden hadn't thought of that. "There are numerous park rangers that I haven't met. Many new ones come and go throughout the tourist season." She stood and hurried to her desk for her laptop, then rushed back to the table. "I can show you the employee page."

Once she had the website up, Zach and Sam stood behind her to look over her shoulder. She scrolled through the employee photos. There were only two men with blond hair. But she couldn't say if either of the men had the same jawline.

"Greg Smith and Patrick Dunbar," Sam said. "I'll look into both of these men and see what I can find."

"Greg Smith sounds like an alias," Zach said.

"I'm sorry I couldn't be more help." Eden had the feeling she was letting everyone down.

"You have given me some more to work with," Sam said as he closed his notebook. "We have Lindsay's height and now we can determine an approximate height for the suspect. We know he can move fast. And he has a square jaw. This will help in asking Lindsay's friends and family if they've ever seen her with a man matching the description."

"I suppose. Like I said, I only saw him for a split second before I turned and ran," Eden said. "I think it's true what you said about memory. Maybe I'm painting a picture that I didn't really see."

"Time will tell." Sam stood. "If I have any more questions, I'll call you. Or if you need anything, give me a call."

While Zach walked Sam out, Eden moved to the living room couch where she sank into the cushions. Taylor jumped onto the back of the couch and nestled near her head while Amber climbed up next to her and settled her head in Eden's lap. She soaked in the comfort the two animals provided, but there was nothing that could solve what ailed her heart.

When Zach walked back into the living room, Eden met his gaze. The soft and tender affection on his face made her want to weep. Or maybe it was the pregnancy that was making her emotional? She needed someone to talk to about the situation. She longed for her mother, who'd died way too young from breast cancer.

The ringing of Zach's phone had him retreating to the kitchen. While she couldn't make out his words, she listened to the soft timbre of his voice. She'd missed this, hearing him in the house, knowing he was close by. She'd missed *him*. But she would never, ever, admit it to him. She couldn't. Not if she didn't want to be hurt all over again.

Zach walked out of the kitchen with the phone still to his ear. "Let me ask," he said to the person on the other line. "Eden, I'm on the phone with Lucy Lopez, one of my colleagues on the task force. She's in town to do some interviews for a case we're working on. Right now, she's at the Keystone Diner and wanted to know if she could bring us dinner."

"Bless her," Eden said, realizing she was hungry. She hadn't kept down her breakfast. Now she understood why. "I would love their butternut squash soup, two hard rolls and a green salad."

Zach grinned. "You heard that?" He listened for a moment, then said, "Yes. I'll take a cheeseburger, fries and a salad. We'll both take ranch."

He gave Lucy the address and then hung up.

Fatigue pulled at Eden. Her eyelids fluttered as she reclined. She could rest her eyes for a few minutes.

The sound of Zach opening the door for Lucy had Eden shaking off her exhaustion. Amber jumped off the couch and scrambled to the door. Taylor remained on the back of the couch, watching as Amber and another dog, a cute brown and white English springer spaniel, ambled into the living room.

"We might need to warm up the soup," a soft female voice said.

Eden pushed herself to sit at the edge of the couch cushion, as a very pretty tall woman with shoulder-length brown hair and brown eyes walked into her house. She wore jeans and a purple lightweight sweater.

Lucy set her bounty on the dining room table and then turned to smile at Eden. "I'm Lucy Lopez. It's nice to meet you, Eden."

Eden stood and took a moment to let the world right itself.

Zach was at her side in an instant, threading his arm around her waist.

Concern bracketed Lucy's eyes. "I heard what happened. I'm here to help."

Instantly liking this woman, Eden smiled. "You brought food. That's a big help. I haven't gone to the grocery store in days."

"I noticed," Zach said with a grin.

Eden didn't want to get into a discussion with him about her taking care of herself. Her well-being was no longer his concern. But then again, maybe it was. As a sheriff's deputy, his job was to protect her. As the father of her child, a child he didn't want, what was his role?

She was so confused and conflicted. Her stomach grumbled. The delicious smells coming from the big bag of food on the table redirected her thoughts.

Zach was quick to help Eden to the dining room chair. Truthfully, she didn't need the help once she got her equilibrium stabilized, but she just couldn't bring herself to push him away, either. It would be rude, she rationalized.

Lucy unpacked the bag, and Zach whisked the soup away to be heated.

After lifting a prayer of thanksgiving for the food, Eden dove into her salad, enjoying the savory taste of the ranch, the crisp lettuce, tomatoes and onions. A few moments later, Zach brought the soup over. She relished the creamy butternut with a hint of turmeric and pepper. Zach sat and ate his hamburger.

Lucy had chicken tenders, fries and salad. She dipped a chicken tender into honey mustard sauce. "This isn't exactly grown-up food, but I'm missing my four-year-old, so I decided to go with her favorite."

Eden immediately leaned forward in eager anticipation. "Tell me more about your daughter."

"Annalise is the light of my life." Tenderness softened Lucy's expression. "She's such a joy. She has some general anxiety, but I got her a therapy dog, a Yorkshire terrier named Fluffy and that has made a world of difference."

"Dogs are such comfort, aren't they?" Her gaze moved to Amber and back to Lucy. "Can I ask you some questions about…being pregnant?"

Lucy's eyes lit up. "Of course."

Eden was grateful that God had brought her someone to talk to. Someone who might be able to help her navigate motherhood. But she wasn't sure anyone could help her navigate a broken heart.

Zach listened as Eden and Lucy talked about pregnancy and motherhood. His gut knotted. Hearing Eden tell Lucy about the baby had been painfully awkward. Even more so when Lucy expressed her delighted congratulations. Lucy had no idea that Zach and Eden were separated, and it hadn't seemed prudent to say so without first talking with Eden. They were going to have to decide how to proceed together.

Anxiety pierced through him. He rubbed at the spot over his heart where a deep ache lodged.

How was he going to deal with being a parent? How was he going to resolve his marriage? Until this morning, he'd been prepared to walk away to allow Eden to find the life she deserved with someone who wanted children. But now they were expecting. How could he walk away? How could he stay?

Needing a little distance from the talk of babies, Zach rose from the table and cleared away the remnants of their meal. Then he headed for the sliding door leading to the backyard. Amber ran ahead of him. "I'll be in the back if either of you needs me."

Eden met his gaze. The distance in her green

eyes stabbed at him. He ducked out. The sun had gone down and the night air turned cool. Stars dotted the sky. The Edison lights he had strung across the back fence provided a warm glow.

He bowed his head. "Lord," he said aloud softly. "I don't know how to do this."

For a long time, he just stared at the stars, letting the night air swirl around him as his anxious thoughts darted in all directions.

Behind him, the slider opened and Lucy's dog, Piper, joined Amber. The two dogs ran across the grass, taking turns chasing each other.

Lucy stepped onto the porch next to him. "Hope you don't mind the company."

"Of course not." Zach glanced inside the house and could see Eden through the kitchen window. She was so heartbreakingly beautiful. Strands of her strawberry blond hair curled around her face. "I needed some fresh air."

"Congratulations again on your impending fatherhood," Lucy said.

He slanted her a glance. Had Eden told her they were separated? His heart crimped with regret. He'd hurt his wife by withholding the fact that he didn't want children. And their big blow-up on Valentine's Day had been the beginning to the end. He hadn't reacted well when she'd suggested they start thinking about children. Tensions had run high between them ever since. And when she'd pressed him for a firm answer, he'd left her because he was too scared to be a dad. Too scared to tell her the truth. Too scared.

Maybe Eden and the baby would be better off without him. Because if he stayed and saw this marriage through, he'd be living his nightmare come true. Every moment would be torture. He'd live in constant fear of something happening to his child. He hated the idea of being the type of parent to smother his child out of his own fear. He wasn't sure he had enough faith to make the fear go away. "It's all a bit overwhelming."

"You'll survive. The day you hold your child in your arms will be your happiest, next to the day you married your wife."

He grimaced. An ache so deep throbbed within his chest. "My marriage is over."

Lucy was silent for a moment. "I don't know what's going on between you two, but I can tell you care for each other."

Caring wouldn't sustain them long-term. At one time he'd have confessed to loving her with his whole heart, but he'd had to close off that part of himself these past two months. There was no room for love in their situation. Love would only make things more complicated and would cloud their judgment. They needed to be practical, and logical. They needed to do what was best for them all. He needed to do what was best for Eden.

But the situation had evolved, Eden was in danger, and he had no idea how to proceed.

And they were expecting. His heart beat so fast the muscle wanted to take flight. How was he supposed to proceed now?

Needing to change the subject away from him and Eden, he sought solace in work. "Are you set for the interviews?"

"I am. I've scheduled several appointments. Tomorrow with Jared Olin's ex-girlfriend, Desiree Weiner. She's been reluctant to talk to us, but I told her we would charge her with impeding an investigation if she didn't cooperate."

"Hopefully she'll give you some good information." They needed a win here. A couple months ago, a low-level weapons trafficker, Petey Pawners, and a then unidentified man were found shot dead at a gas station not far from where the two men had had a shoot-out with police. Then last month the John Doe was finally identified as Keystone local, thirty-four-year-old Jared Olin. "An interview has been set up later this week with the man's family."

Lucy nodded. "We should be able to wrap this up by next weekend."

Amber raced past Zach toward the back sliding door that led into the kitchen. Her deep growl sent a shudder through Zach.

Was Eden in trouble?

FIVE

With a scream lodged in her throat, Eden stared at the towering man wearing a black knit mask covering everything but his eyes, which were concealed by dark sunglasses. Was this Lindsay's killer? In his hand, he held a gun aimed at her heart. She'd come out of the kitchen to find him standing in the middle of her living room and her front door wide open. Placing a protective hand over her tummy she froze in place.

The gun wavered in his hand. Was he as scared as she was?

Amber's nails clicked rapidly along the linoleum of the kitchen floor. The assailant's attention snapped toward the sound as Amber raced into the living room.

The intruder grabbed for Eden at the same moment Amber lunged at him.

"No!" Eden screamed and darted out of the assailant's reach. She had to protect her baby.

Amber latched on to the forearm of the gloved hand holding the gun. The assailant let out a guttural scream, desperately trying to shake off the black Lab.

Then Zach tackled the intruder and took him to the ground. The gun flew out of the assailant's hand and slid under the couch.

Lucy pulled Eden out of harm's way and took a protective stance in front of her with Piper at her side, barking for all she was worth. Lucy removed her weapon from a holster at her back, but with Zach and the masked man wrestling on the carpet, she clearly couldn't take aim. Amber still had her teeth around the man's arm and was stepping on Zach to gain purchase, hindering his movements.

"Out," Zach yelled the command for Amber to release her bite.

Amber immediately let go but stayed close, snarling and barking.

Zach and the assailant grappled on the floor, each trying to get the upper hand. Eden held her breath, praying Zach would prevail.

Planting his booted foot in Zach's chest, the masked man shoved him away enough to scramble to his feet and bolt for the door.

Lucy raised her gun, but Amber jumped at the fleeing intruder, forcing Lucy to lower her weapon.

"Stay," Zach ordered Amber. The dog whined as Lucy and Piper ran out the door behind the masked man.

Zach got to his feet and turned to Eden. "Are you okay?"

"I'm fine." But he did not look fine. His lip was split, and red splotches appeared on his face. One of his hands wrapped around his ribs.

Distress arched through Eden. "You're hurt."

He waved off her concern as Lucy and Piper returned.

"He ran down the street and I lost him. I didn't want to risk him firing randomly and hitting a civilian," Lucy said. "I've called for backup."

"Lucy, keep her safe and find the gun." Zach raced out the front door with Amber at his side.

Eden's heart beat so fast she thought it might burst from her chest.

Piper sniffed along the edges of the couch.

Lucy dropped to her knees on the floor and looked under the couch. "Found it." But she didn't grab it. She stood and glanced around before she grabbed a pencil off the desk and hurried to crouch by the couch again. Using the tip of the pencil, she snagged the handgun through the trigger guard and brought it out. "Do you have a paper bag?"

Eden's legs were rubbery, but she hurried to the kitchen and found a small brown paper bag that she used for lunches and handed it to Lucy.

"I'm not sure we'll get prints off this," Lucy said as she slipped the gun into the bag. "He had gloves on."

"Just like he had when he strangled Lindsay," Eden said.

"That's assuming it's the same man," Lucy said.

"It has to be, right?" she said.

Eden sent up a prayer that Zach would be able to apprehend the attacker and end this nightmare.

Amber tracked the scent of the attacker down the street for several minutes. Zach hurried behind his K-9 partner, keeping an eye out for the intruder. The blow he'd taken to the ribs ached. His face hurt and his ego was bruised.

The streetlights along the quiet residential area illuminated round pools of light on the sidewalks but left shifting shadows in the yards of the neighborhood. The assailant could be crouched behind Mrs. Longfield's rosebushes. Or using the Smiths' garbage cans for cover.

Bypassing the roses and the garbage cans, Amber led Zach to a house around the corner at the end of the dead-end street. The Lab alerted at the front door of the two-story craftsman home. Had the man they were chasing entered the house? Concerned for his neighbors, Zach hurried up the porch steps and banged on the door. No one answered. He tried the doorknob. Locked.

Peering through the front windows, he could see the outline of a couch and side chair through the darkened interior. A potted plant on a stand stood near the front door. But he detected no human presence. Was the assailant the home-owner?

With caution tripping down his spine, he led Amber around to the backyard, thinking maybe the guy had gone through the house and out the back door, possibly over the back fence.

But Amber seemed confused. She picked up the trigger scent and then lost it all over the back porch, the backyard and at the fence to the neighbors. The suspect had clearly been here at one time and had possibly escaped over the wooden fence.

Wanting to be sure the homeowners were safe, Zach knocked on the back door. Still no answer.

Taking out his phone, he texted the task force tech analyst, asking if she was available.

A moment later Zach's phone rang. The caller ID said it was Cheyenne Chen.

"Hey, Cheyenne, I have a huge favor to ask," Zach said into the phone as he and Amber walked toward the front of the house. "The boss said I could use task force resources, and I need you to tell me who lives at this address." He relayed the numbers and the name of the street to Cheyenne. "There's no name on the mailbox, just the numbers."

"Sure thing, Zach," Cheyenne said. "You just caught me. I was about to leave. But this should only take me a moment."

Zach could hear Cheyenne's fingers typing away on her computer keyboard. A moment later, she came back on the line and said, "The house is owned by a Jon and Julie Fielding."

Zach had never met the couple. "Are there any photos you can find of him?"

"His South Dakota driver's license. I'll text it to you."

A second later his phone dinged with an incoming text. He looked at the image of a dark-haired, dark-eyed man with a full beard. His weight put him on the thinner side, but he was six feet tall. Zach tried to picture the masked man whom he'd fought with. He was six feet but heavier, and more athletic than Jon Fielding's description. Could Jon Fielding have gained muscle?

But why would a married, suburban man go after Lindsay Nash? What was their connection?

Zach hated to ask more of Cheyenne, but he did anyway. "Sorry to keep you late, but could you see if you can locate the whereabouts of Jon and Julie Fielding?"

"Not a problem. I can try," Cheyenne said. "It may take me a bit. I'll ring you when I have more information. Stay safe."

Zach's next call was to his colleague at the sheriff's department, Sam Powell. He needed to know that Eden had been threatened again—and this time the attacker had gone so far as to find her at home.

* * *

Eden paced the living room waiting to hear from Zach. Had he found the intruder? Lindsay's *killer*. Was Zach okay? With every tick of the clock, her anxiety ratcheted up like someone was twisting screws. The tightness in her chest was nearly unbearable.

Lucy was on her phone in the kitchen. Eden heard her say "boss" and figured she must be talking to the task force leader.

A knock at the front door had her heart jamming into her throat.

Then she heard a key being fitted into the lock, and a moment later the door opened. Amber and Zach rushed in.

It took all of Eden's willpower not to rush to her husband, throw her arms around his neck and kiss him. Relief that he was okay flooded Eden's veins, and she sat down on the couch to keep from crumbling to the floor. Amber came over and kissed her, licking her face and nuzzling against her.

"What do you know about the Fieldings?" Zach asked.

Eden cocked her head. "Julie Fielding? We're friends. Sort of. We've gone hiking together a few times." Eden's stomach knotted. "Is Julie okay?"

"Amber led me to their property, but no one appeared to be home. The house was dark and no one answered when I knocked. Whoever broke in here and held a gun on you went to the Fielding house and was either hiding inside or escaped over the back fence."

Confusion swirled through Eden's brain. "Julie's husband's name is Jon. But he's got very dark hair and a beard. At least, the last time I saw him." Her mind whirled. "Or maybe he put on a blond wig when he killed Lindsay. But why would Jon Fielding want to hurt Lindsay Nash?"

"Sam will arrive soon. We need to find out if there's a connection between the Fieldings and Lindsay," Zach said. "Maybe Cheyenne could tap into Lindsay's social media accounts and telephone records to find a link."

"I can call Cheyenne and ask her to do that," Lucy said. She retreated to the kitchen.

Eden almost joined her. The tension rolling off Zach buffeted against her like waves crashing into a cliff. She'd never seen him in work mode before. Witnessing him and the assailant fighting had been overwhelming, scary even. Though Zach didn't scare her, she was afraid for him. For the danger of his job.

She'd never had a front-row seat to the reality of what Zach, or her father, had faced out in the field. She couldn't imagine doing their job without faith in God above. Faith and hope in the goodness and sovereignty of God made the uncertainty of their chosen professions bearable.

Shaking her head to dislodge the thoughts, she focused on what Zach was saying.

"What can you tell me about Mrs. Fielding?" Zach sat on the coffee table across from Eden, their knees touching.

"To be honest, Julie's a little afraid of Jon," Eden confessed. "I don't want to talk out of turn, but Julie confided in me that Jon can be very controlling. He alienated her family and cost her her friends."

Zach's hands curled into fists on his knees. "He was abusive?"

Sensing his upset on behalf of her friend had tenderness welling inside of her. She tamped it down. "Julie never said anything about physical abuse, but that doesn't mean it couldn't have happened. He was emotionally abusive. She told me a few stories that led me to think he gaslights her. And he keeps her on a tight budget."

"Do you know where Jon and Julie are now?" Zach asked.

"I haven't seen Julie in several days," Eden said. "I counseled her to leave him the last time we met. I gave her information on the local women's shelter. And I talked to her about obtaining a protection order to keep Jon away."

Zach raised an eyebrow. "Did she leave him?"

"Not that I know of." Heaviness settled on her heart. "She was very noncommittal. She was reluctant to do something that might set him off and make things worse. I called and left a message last week asking if she was okay and if she needed help, and she texted back saying everything was fine. She didn't respond when I asked if she wanted to go for a hike on my day off this week."

"Can you text her now and see if she is with Jon?"

"Of course." Hurrying across the room to where she left her phone charging on the desk, she quickly texted Julie.

Just checking in. Is everything okay? Where are you and Jon? I noticed your house is dark.

Sitting back on the couch, Eden held the phone against her thigh. "It could be a while before she texts back."

Lucy walked into the living room. "Cheyenne's going to comb through Lindsay's social media accounts to see if there's any mention of a boyfriend. She's also going to ask Daniel to make a warrant request for Lindsay's phone records."

A knock at the door jolted through Eden. Zach patted her knee before he rose and opened the door for the sheriff department's investigator Sam Powell.

"Seems our suspect is pretty determined to quiet you," Sam said to Eden as he sat at the dining room table and took out his notebook and a pen.

"Yes," Eden agreed with a shiver. "But he could have shot me. Why didn't he?"

"Killing someone in cold blood takes more courage than it seems in the heat of the moment," Sam replied. "I've seen it happen before."

"I'm thankful he froze," Zach said. "But I have to make sure he doesn't get another chance."

"Tell me about the Fieldings," Sam instructed.

Eden repeated what she'd told Zach and Lucy. Zach added how Amber had tracked the suspect to the house and around to the backyard fence.

"It sounds like you all are on top of this," Sam said after Lucy filled him in on what their tech analyst, Cheyenne, was doing. "In the morning, we will canvas the neighborhood to see if we can find any witnesses, or porch video cameras that give us a glimpse of our perpetrator. And I'll follow up with the Fieldings at their house. I've looked into the two park rangers. Still working on tracking their whereabouts. We should have more information on them soon. I haven't reached Lindsay's family yet. I've sent local police officers to break the news. I'll try again tomorrow to talk to them myself. And I'll be sure to ask if they know of who Lindsay might have been dating or had any issues with. Tomorrow I will also interview her friends here in town."

"Let me know if I can help." Zach walked Sam out the door.

"There's not a lot more we can do tonight."

Lucy whistled, and her springer spaniel, Piper, scrambled to her feet from where she lay at the back door. "We'll head back to the hotel and then check in with you in the morning."

Eden jumped up. "You don't have to go. We have a spare bedroom."

It wasn't that Eden didn't feel safe with Zach, but if Lucy stayed with them, then they would all be protected. Even though her marriage was ending, Eden didn't want anything to happen to Zach. He needed to be around to be a father to their child. She just had to believe that once the baby came he would want to be a part of their child's life. Even if only part-time. Her heart wept with sorrow. She missed her mother, thinking how awful it would've been had she not had those years with her.

"Yes, please stay," Zach said as he walked back into the room. "I'll be camping out here on the couch in case the intruder comes back. The spare bedroom will be empty."

Lucy's gaze bounced between Eden and Zach. She seemed to be contemplating their request. "I need to run to the hotel and grab my bag."

"We'll go with you," Eden said quickly. Lucy could be a buffer. "Zach needs to pick up his car from his rental house."

"True enough," Zach said. "And I want to grab some of my things."

Eden was pretty sure he had everything he

needed here at the house, but she wasn't going to quibble.

"Okay, then." Lucy and Piper headed to the front door.

Eden grabbed her purse and kept her phone in her hand as she followed Lucy out the door, with Amber and Zach bringing up the rear.

By the time they made the stop at the motel for Lucy to grab her suitcase and then at Zach's rental so he could gather what he needed, Eden was exhausted.

Back at the house, Eden showed Lucy to the guest room. Her gaze swept over the stack of boxes she'd packed full of Zach's things and a pang stung her heart. "The bed has clean sheets. There's a bathroom across the hall."

Lucy set her suitcase down. "I'm here if you need to talk."

Giving her a smile, Eden said, "I appreciate that." She backed out of the room and hurried to the primary suite.

A moment later, she heard a scratching on the other side of the door. She opened it, and Amber pushed past her to jump up on the bed.

Sitting next to the Lab, she rubbed Amber behind the ears. "I think you should be out in the living room with Zach."

From the doorway, Zach said, "I think she should stay here with you. She'll alert if anyone is skulking around the outside of the house."

Eden's heart thumped. She appreciated Zach being so protective and careful. He was a good man. Just apparently not the right man for her. She put a hand to her stomach. Yet, they were having a child together. Confusion and anxiety swirled through her, making the room tilt. She couldn't do this right now. Not with her emotions running so high. "Thank you. I'll feel safe with her here. Good night, Zach."

Hurt flashed in his gaze, but he nodded and backed out of the room, shutting the door behind him.

Leaving Amber curled in a ball on the edge of the king-size bed, Eden went about her nightly routine while holding in the sorrow of letting go of Zach. She changed into a comfortable pair of lightweight silk pajama bottoms and a matching top.

A buzzing drew her from the bathroom back to the bedroom, where she'd left her phone on the bedside table. She quickly grabbed it and read the text from Julie Fielding.

Yes, everything is okay. Thanks to you for making me realize that I needed to leave Jon. It took me a while, but I packed my bags and left. I filed that protection order you told me about. I'm at the shelter now and will try to reconnect with my family.

Putting her hand over her heart, Eden sat on the edge of the bed. Amber crawled closer and put her snout on her thigh. Julie was safe. Eden debated waiting until morning to show Julie's response to Zach but then decided he'd want to know now. She left the bedroom with Amber at her heels.

The guest room door was open, but the door to the bath was closed. Eden decided she would tell Lucy after Zach. In the living room, Zach stood at the front window in lounge pants and a long-sleeved shirt.

He must've seen her and Amber's reflection in the window because he turned, and said, "Can't sleep?"

"Haven't tried yet." She hurried forward with her hand extended, offering him the phone. "Julie texted back."

Zach took the phone and read the text. "That puts a little different spin on things."

"How so?"

"An emotionally abusive man whose wife finally left him and filed an order of protection against him while she stays at a women's shelter could be capable of most anything," he said.

"But wouldn't he go after Julie, his wife, instead of someone like Lindsay? What was their connection?" She thought for a minute. "Her killer was in the park before hours—had Lindsay let him in? And *was* the man Jon Fielding in disguise?"

"Could be Jon Fielding was having an affair with Lindsay Nash."

"But if that was the case," Eden countered, "then why kill her? Wouldn't he be free to keep seeing her with Julie out of the picture? Oh, wait," she added as she recalled that day. "Lindsay argued with her killer right before he attacked her. If it was Jon, maybe he snapped?" She shivered at the thought.

"That's a mystery we have yet to solve," Zach said. "I'm going to forward this text to Cheyenne and Sam."

Eden waited until he'd taken care of that before reaching for her phone.

Zach took her hand and led her to the couch. "We need to talk."

With her heart stuttering, Eden sat on the edge of the cushion. "What is there to say? We're having a baby, and you don't want to be a father."

"It's not so cut-and-dried." Zach ran a hand through his hair, shifting the brown strands into disarray. "I'm still processing what this means for us. For our future."

"I don't think we have a future." They didn't share the dream of children. Of building a family together. As much as it hurt her to say the words, she had to accept the reality. They both had to. And the quicker they did, the less painful in the long run.

"I can work past my feelings and adapt," he said.

"Adapt?" Sadness seeped through her, chilling her bones. Her heart clenched at his willingness to try. He'd be doing the right thing, but his heart wouldn't be in it. "No. I want more than you adapting. Our child deserves more than you adapting." She tugged her hand from his. "Let's just get through the current situation and then we can figure out how to proceed with dismantling our marriage."

Tears burned the backs of her eyes as she stood and brushed past him.

That hadn't gone the way he'd hoped. Zach scrubbed a hand over his face as he watched Eden disappear down the hall. Her strawberry blond hair hung down her back and swayed with her quick steps. The wedding ring he'd noticed earlier was still on her finger. Despite her words, she still wore the symbol of their marriage. He was so confused. He curbed the urge to go after her, to hash out their future now before more time passed and more distance gaped between them. He'd wanted to let Eden know he planned to be there for her and the baby. But he was terrified to his very core. What if he failed his child? What if something happened to their baby while in his care?

Movement in his peripheral vision had him jumping to his feet, his body ready for an attack.

"Whoa," Lucy said, holding her hands up,

palms out. She'd changed into sweatpants and a zipped hoodie. "I didn't mean to scare you."

The tension left his body in a whoosh. He waved off her words. "No worries. Did you need something?"

"Just leaving the bathroom," she said. "I didn't mean to overhear your conversation."

"Can I ask you a personal question?" From what he'd heard, Lucy had never married and was raising her daughter with the help of her mother. Asking about the child's father would be crossing a line. "Is it difficult being a parent?"

A soft smile touched Lucy's lips. "It is. In so many ways. But it's also wonderful."

"I don't—" Zach's words were cut off by Piper barking.

From the back bedroom, Amber also barked.

A loud explosion rocked the house.

SIX

Heart jackhammering in his chest, Zach sprinted across the living room toward the hall.

Toward Eden.

The echo of the explosion rang in his ears, tempering the barking of the dogs. The primary suite door jerked open. Amber's frantic barks and growls bounced off the hallway walls as Amber and Eden raced out of the room.

Eden, wearing silk pj's in a floral pattern that covered her from neck to ankle, launched herself into Zach's arms. "What happened?"

"I don't know." Zach held her tight, reveling in the feel of her. This woman. His wife. Though not for much longer. For a moment he was over-whelmed with the enormity of the future, but the present situation needed to be dealt with. He needed to get her and their unborn child to safety.

He set her away from him, grabbed her by the hand and tugged her into the living room. Eden scooped up the cat and cuddled her close to her chest.

Lucy was gone, and the front door stood open.

Outside, Piper barked. Concern for Lucy tugged at him. Was the officer in trouble? Pulling Eden and Taylor with him, Zach raced out the front door with Amber at their heels.

The garage where it shared a wall with the primary suite was on fire. Flames licked the sides and shot into the air. Lucy stood on the sidewalk, phone to her ear as she relayed the emergency to 911 while holding an agitated Piper by the leash.

"Oh," Eden breathed out. "Thankfully my car is still in the employee parking lot at the park."

A small favor for which Zach was grateful. But he was more grateful Eden was safe. "Stay close."

He mentally cataloged the many tools and boxes of storage that were being destroyed as they watched. All of it could be replaced.

The sounds of sirens punctuated the night.

Acrid smoke filled the air. Zach tugged both women farther away and called to the dogs. "Heel."

Within moments, the fire department and fellow deputies from the Pennington County Sheriff's Department arrived on the scene. Thankful for the additional law enforcement personnel, Zach left Eden in Lucy's care, confident Eden would be safe with the officer, as he consulted with the fire chief. "This had to be arson."

Chief Hendrix barely spared him a glance as he watched his firefighters hosing down the remains of the garage. "The arson investigation team will determine whether that's true or not."

Zach needed to be looped in on the investigation to know if this was the work of Lindsay Nash's killer. The arsonist's intent had been to burn Eden in her bed. The part of the garage that was on fire would surely have spread through the primary suite. If not for the lawnmower's gas tank inside the garage exploding and warning them the killer might have succeeded. Unease slithered down his spine. "You should have your men hose down the rest of the house. I wouldn't be surprised if there isn't more accelerant splash about."

Chief Hendrickson stared at him long and hard and seemed to come to his own conclusion that Zach was right before getting on his radio. "Hose down the whole house. We have suspected arson."

Zach hustled back to where Lucy and Eden were now talking with Sam and two other Pennington sheriff's deputies.

"The fire arson investigation team will be notified," Zach told Sam.

Sam nodded. He was dressed in civil clothes. He must have been home when he received the call. "Until then you'll need to find a new safe place to lay low."

"Good thing I didn't give up my rental," Zach said.

"Can we go in and pack some things?" Eden asked.

The paleness of her face worried Zach.

"Once the fire chief gives an all clear," Sam said. "You should be able to go in."

"How long will that be?" Lucy asked.

"As long as it takes. Most likely tomorrow," Sam said. "I didn't catch your name."

Zach stepped in to make the introduction. "This is Officer Lucy Lopez. She works with me on the task force." He gestured to his fellow deputy sheriff. "Sam Powell."

Sam held out his hand and shook Lucy's hand. "Good to meet you, Lucy."

"Likewise," Lucy replied.

Turning to Zach, Sam said, "I'll stay in touch with the arson investigation and keep you informed."

Zach noticed Eden shivering in the cool night air. The pj's she wore weren't meant to keep out the cold. His instinct was to wrap her in his arms again to hold her tight and warm her up. Instead, his gaze went to his vehicle parked in the driveway and getting soaked by the fire department hoses. But Lucy's Fargo K-9 Unit vehicle was parked down the street.

He addressed his task force team member. "Maybe you ladies should sit in your car?"

Lucy's gaze snapped to Zach. "Excuse me?"

Zach winced. Lucy, a great cop handpicked for the Dakota Gun Task Force, didn't need to be coddled. Neither did Eden. "It would be warmer and less exposed."

Lucy looked like she wanted to argue. But then her gaze searched the growing crowd of homeowners who had come out to see what was happening. Lucy nodded and said to Eden, "He's right. You're too visible standing out here."

Eden's eyes widened as her gaze jumped from Lucy to Zach and back. "I hadn't thought of that." Without hesitation or waiting for Lucy, Eden turned and hustled to Lucy's vehicle, climbed into the back seat and scrunched down. Zach released Amber, who hustled to hop into the vehicle beside her.

Lucy, with Piper at her side, took a step, then paused to level Zach with a formidable scowl. "I don't like being sidelined."

"You're doing me a solid," Zach told her, needing her to understand his priority was Eden's well-being. "Eden will be safe with you."

Seeming mollified, Lucy gave a sharp nod, strode to the small SUV and let Piper into the back.

"Why don't you all head to your rental," Sam said, gesturing to where Lucy sat in the driver's seat of her vehicle with Eden, cradling Taylor the cat in her arms, and the dogs in the back. "When we get the all clear, I'll let you know."

"Thanks. Please keep me in the loop." Zach was torn between wanting to have Amber trace whatever scents she could find and his need to be with his wif—with Eden and their child.

His duty was to protect his family. With two attacks at home in one night, Zach feared this killer was desperate.

With trepidation, Eden moved past Zach as he held open the door to enter the small cottage that he'd moved into after they'd decided to separate. Amber rushed in and went straight to her water bowl. Lucy's dog Piper joined Amber. The two dogs couldn't have been more different. One sleek and regal and the other stout and sturdy.

Tenderness welled in Eden for the two animals. She'd never really been much of a dog person before Amber, but now she couldn't imagine life without a canine. She set Taylor down, and the cat immediately jumped onto the back of the couch where she could watch the dogs and humans.

Eden looked around the cottage, noting the empty take-out containers and dirty dishes sitting on the coffee table. Clothes had been strewn about as if Zach had just literally walked in at the end of his shift, taken off his uniform and slung it over the back of the chair. A basket full of what she assumed were clean clothes sat on the couch, with some of the clothes spilling out as if he'd dug through them. Her heart squeezed in her chest, but she tried not to be affected by the sight of how her usually tidy husband had turned into the quintessential bachelor.

Lucy followed Eden inside.

Zach shut the door behind him and moved quickly to the couch, picking up the clothes and throwing them into the basket. He turned and stilled as if caught, his expression one of vulnerability. Eden's heart squeezed tighter still.

"I'm sorry to say this is a one bedroom," he said.

"That's fine," Lucy said. "Piper and I will go to the hotel. We all need a good night's rest."

"Maybe I should go to the hotel with Lucy," Eden offered as a panicked flutter knocked in her chest.

"No," Zach was quick to say. "If you go to the hotel, then I will, too."

Eden grimaced. He was taking this protection thing very seriously. Because of her? Because of the baby? Because it was his job? She wanted to believe it was because of her and the baby.

However, she knew in her heart that Zach was a man of honor, so his reasons had to be a little bit of all three, which made the situation much more difficult. His integrity would demand he stay married to her and be a father, even though that was not what he wanted.

She did not want to be a statistic. But she also didn't want to live a life where he would grow to resent her and their child. They were stuck between bad choices.

Weariness settled on her shoulders, and she didn't even realize she was listing to the side until Zach scooped her up with an arm under her knees and an arm around her back.

She blinked away the pull of sleepiness and batted at his shoulder. "What are you doing?"

Ignoring her question, Zach asked, "Have you had any water today?"

Ah. Of course. She was dehydrated. She knew better. How many times had she warned visitors to the park to keep hydrated? Not a good thing for her or the baby. Since getting the big news, she hadn't had a single moment to do any research on pregnancy and what to expect beyond what she'd learned from Lucy. She would have to make time to gather more information. "Not much."

"I'm on it." Lucy moved into the kitchen.

"Put me down," Eden insisted.

Zach grunted, then set her gingerly on his couch. The thing was hard, nothing like their soft comfy leather couch at home. "You think our house will be saved?"

A pained expression crossed his face. "I hope so. I think the fire department contained the fire to the garage. But there might be water damage or smoke damage we'll need to deal with before the place is livable again."

She wanted to weep. Her whole life was going up in smoke all around her.

Lucy returned with a glass of water. Eden forced herself to drink it all. Her stomach wanted to rebel and expel the liquid and the remnants of her dinner. But she kept her lips pressed together and continued to swallow long after she finished the glass of water. When the nausea finally abated, she said, "I need to sleep."

Zach held out his hand. "You can take the bedroom. I'll stay here in the living room."

Eden stared at his strong and capable hand. There had been a time when she would have gladly held on and never let go, but that time had passed. She had to learn to rely on herself again as she had done before meeting and marrying Zach. She rose without taking his hand. She walked over to Lucy. "I'm sorry."

The other woman looked startled. "For what?"

"This is all such a mess." Despite knowing she didn't bear responsibility for Lindsay's death, remorse still oozed through her for dragging Lucy into the chaos.

Lucy put a hand on her shoulder and stared into her eyes. "You have nothing to apologize for. You need to rest. You are stronger than you think." Lucy stepped back. "I'll return first thing in the morning."

Eden liked this woman and was grateful for her presence. There was something very forthright and intense about Lucy. "Thank you. I'll say good night, then."

Eden made it to the bedroom on her own and waited a beat, but this time Amber didn't join her. Taylor wound through her legs before jumping up onto the bed, which was covered in a dark green comforter. Fluffy pillows beckoned. The room was spartan. A suitcase lay on the floor with more clothes spilling out of it.

Zach hadn't made this place into a home for himself.

She wasn't sure how to feel about his lack of settling into the rental. Had he been hoping they would reconcile? Was that something that was even on the table?

Taylor jumped off the bed and disappeared beneath the edge of the bed frame. The cat liked to sleep in dark, tight spaces. Eden climbed between the sheets and lay down, hugging a pillow to her chest and breathing in the scent of her soon-to-be ex-husband that would be forever marked on her senses.

How were they going to survive the future without more heartache?

SEVEN

The next morning, Zach dressed in haste when he heard noises coming from the living area of the cottage. Apparently, Eden had risen and left the bedroom while he was in the shower in the guest bathroom. He'd expected her to sleep in after all that had occurred.

But maybe, like him, she hadn't slept well.

His mind tormented him by replaying the day and evening. There'd been too many close calls on Eden's life. First in the park when she witnessed Lindsay's murder, and then when the attacker went after Eden. Then the killer showed up at their house with a gun, escaped and no doubt came back to burn down the place. Zach's nerves were shredded.

Wearing a fresh sheriff's uniform, he hurried into the kitchen to find her making eggs and toast. She was dressed in lightweight slacks and a blue shirt with tiny white flowers. She looked fresh, young and vulnerable. His heart ached with tenderness.

The soft morning light kissed her hair with fire. Her petal soft skin glistened, and she had applied a bit of gloss to her full, kissable lips. He mentally gave himself a head slap. He shouldn't still find her so attractive, but he did. And if he was honest with himself, he always would.

They would be forever linked by the child she carried.

Coffee gurgled in the pot. A welcome distraction. He headed over to pour himself a cup. "Eden, you don't have to cook for me. I should be cooking for you."

"Nonsense," she said. "It's important we both eat."

He grunted in agreement as he fought back the hurt invading his chest that she wasn't cooking because she still cared for him. Of course, she didn't. He'd dashed her hopes and crushed her dreams with his refusal to want children. Ah, but the joke was on him. He had no control over the circumstances, and they were having a child. He sought for something to say but came up empty.

"Plus," she continued, "I have an appointment downtown. So we need to get a move on."

This was news to him. With the mug of hot coffee in hand, he faced his wife. "What's downtown?"

"I made an appointment with the ob-gyn the doctor at the emergency room suggested," she replied. "They had a cancellation this morning. And they can fit me in."

His chest tightened. This was becoming very real. This would be the first of many appointments with the obstetrician.

Glad she was being proactive about her and the baby's health care, he set his mug on the dining table and then moved to the refrigerator to grab a carton of orange juice with calcium. That would be good for the baby, wouldn't it? There was so much he didn't know and would have to learn. The thought was daunting. A flutter of panic hit him, but he tamped it down as he poured two glasses of orange juice.

Eden set the food onto plates and carried them to the table. "We kind of need to hustle."

She could be just as bossy as him at times.

Another trait that had drawn him to her. He liked that she was strong, opinionated and self-assured.

"Aye, aye, Captain," he said with a smile.

They made quick work of eating the delicious breakfast and cleaning up. With Amber in tow, wearing her K-9 vest, they drove the few blocks to the ob-gyn's office on the edge of town. Zach kept an eye out for anyone who seemed too interested in them. None of the neighbors or the drivers of the few cars that passed by paid them any attention.

Yet, the hairs at the base of his neck quivered

with awareness. Amber showed no signs of alerting or distress. The dog was intuitive when it came to threat assessment. He forced himself to relax.

At the clinic, he opened the door for Eden and Amber to enter the modern new building that housed a premier medical center. They took the elevator to the fourth floor and followed the signs to the obstetrician's wing.

Inside the waiting room, two other couples were sitting in comfy, cushioned chairs. Both mothers-to-be looked like they were in the last trimester of their pregnancy.

Both fathers smiled at Zach and gave a nod.

He felt like he'd just entered a new club that only other fathers could understand. His heart rate sped up with an uncomfortable trill of excitement deep inside of him that made him want to turn tail and run.

But he needed to stay strong and not let the trepidation threaten to overwhelm him.

Eden approached the front desk and gave her name. She was given forms to fill out. He followed her to a set of chairs near the window.

He stretched out his legs. Amber lay down between their feet.

Eden quickly filled out the forms.

When she was done, she tapped the edge of the pen against the clipboard. A clear sign she was agitated.

He put his hand over her hand holding the pen and leaned in close to whisper in her ear, "It's going to be okay."

She slanted him a glance that was filled with irritation and confusion. "How?" she whispered back.

He didn't have an answer. There was so much they needed to discuss. But this wasn't the time or place. Staying focused on the moment was all he could do for now.

The door to the exam offices opened, and a nurse stepped out. "Eden Kelcey?"

Eden rose. "That's me."

Zach's heart thumped. Hearing his last name attached to her always filled him with pride. And soon their child would also be a Kelcey. The enormity of it all burned at the back of his eyes. *Get a grip.* Now was not the time to go soft and emotional. He was here for Eden and the baby. *Stay focused.* He and Amber stood and followed her to the door.

Eden turned and put up a hand. "I'd prefer if you'd wait out here."

The request burrowed deep with stinging force. But he understood. He had told her he didn't want children, so it made sense she'd think he wouldn't want to be included. But he didn't want to be left out. "I'd like to be there for the ultrasound."

The nurse smiled sympathetically. "First, a

physical exam and some blood work. You'll have plenty of time to see the baby later, Papa."

Given no choice, and wanting to respect Eden's privacy, Zach stepped back. "I'll be right here waiting."

Eden gave him a grateful smile, though he could tell the edges wobbled and her eyes glistened slightly. She was really nervous. Regret that he couldn't be there to reassure her swamped him. Because she didn't want him to be with her. His own fault.

She disappeared behind the door. Not quite sure what to do, he returned to the chair he'd occupied earlier. Amber sat on her haunches and leaned into him as if she sensed he needed some comfort as they settled in to wait.

Eden made it halfway through the exam before she started to cry as she explained to the doctor the recent events and how she discovered she was pregnant.

Dr. Prama, a woman in her sixties with dark salted hair and big brown eyes, was sympathetic. "Dear, it's normal for new moms to be emotional, especially with so much happening. The stress isn't good for you or the baby."

Taking the woman's words at face value, that the hormones were primarily to blame and were compounded by the danger, helped to ease some of the heartache wrenching through Eden.

Though she knew her tears stemmed from sorrow and anxiety. The future seemed bleak without Zach.

When the exam was over and vials of blood were collected, the doctor said, "Everything looks good. I'll go run a couple of quick tests and be right back. Then we can listen to the baby's heartbeat."

Excitement raced along her limbs. Zach should be here at her side. She couldn't deny him the opportunity to hear their child's heartbeat. He could refuse, but he'd asked about the ultrasound so he had to be at least curious, if not excited. "Is there any chance you could send my husband back?" Eden asked. "I'm sure we both have some questions for you."

"Of course. You can get dressed. I'll only need access to your stomach," the doctor said as she took vials of blood and other fluids out of the exam room.

Eden made quick work of changing back into her clothes. She balled up the exam gown and tossed it in a hamper in the corner.

A few moments later, there was a knock on the door.

"Come in," Eden called out.

The door opened, and Zach and Amber stepped in. Zach kept Amber close when it appeared the dog wanted to roam around the room sniffing.

"What did the doctor say? And what do you think of her?" Concern lit Zach's dark brown eyes.

"She seems to think everything's going as it should," Eden said. "She has a sweet demeanor but yet very competent."

"Competent is good," Zach said.

He appeared ill at ease as his gaze bounced over the room and snagged on the wall photos of the gestational periods of the fetus. His face grew a little pale.

She patted the exam table next to her. "Zach, sit with me."

He moved to the exam table but didn't sit, even though she scooted over to make room. "What are we waiting for?"

"She has some tests that she wanted to run before we hear the heartbeat," she told him.

"Tests? Is this normal?" Then her words seemed to sink in. "Heartbeat?"

Bemused by his concern and the vulnerability in his tone, she laid a hand on his arm. "Your guess is as good as mine on if this is normal. I've never done this before."

He let out a laugh that sounded more strangled than his normal chuckle. "Of course not."

"And she said heartbeat."

"Wow."

It took of all Eden's willpower not to lean in for a kiss. They should be celebrating this milestone in their lives. But instead, there was a pall over the experience because this wasn't what he'd wanted for his life.

Another knock sounded on the door, which caused both Eden and Zach to jump.

"Come in," Eden said.

The door opened and Dr. Prama walked back in. "I've confirmed what the emergency room told you. You are indeed nine weeks pregnant. Are you taking the prenatal vitamins?"

Eden nodded. "I took them this morning. Is it okay if I go back to work?"

At the same time, Zach asked, "She should rest, right?"

Throwing him an annoyed glance, Eden said, "Zach—"

He held up a hand. "Let the doctor answer."

"I would say you're safe to go back to work as long as you don't do anything too strenuous or stressful," the doctor said. "However, resting as much as possible would be good, as well."

Eden gritted her teeth. She and Zach couldn't both be right. But she decided to let it go. Now was not the time to argue with Zach in front of the doctor.

"Now, Mom and Dad, let's hear your baby's heartbeat."

A shrill noise filled the air.

Dread shuddered through Eden. "It's the fire alarm!"

EIGHT

The sound of the fire alarm rang in Zach's ears. His first instinct was to grab Eden and rush out of the building. But there were others, civilians, who also needed to be evacuated. He had to keep his emotions in check and rely on his training. Yes, Eden and their child were a priority, but so were the other mothers-to-be, the fathers, the staff and other people in the building. And he was wearing his uniform, so everyone would look to him for guidance.

He hustled Eden and Dr. Prama out of the exam room and into the lobby.

"All right, everybody, file out in an orderly fashion to the emergency stairwell," he said in a calm voice. He snaked an arm around Eden. "You go out with everybody else. Down the staircase. Stay with people."

"What about you?" she asked, her green eyes wide with worry.

"I need to make sure that the building is cleared

safely." He nudged her toward the exit along with all the other people.

She grabbed his arm and pulled him away from the throng of soon-to-be parents and staff as they fled out of the obstetrician's office door and headed down the hall to the staircase at a quick pace.

"I will help evacuate the building," she told him. "I'm trained for situations like this."

Frustration reared in his system. "Evacuating a park is a different situation than evacuating a building."

"I'm sure the procedures and protocols are similar," she told him with a frown. "You want to waste time standing here arguing or should we work our way down each floor to make sure all the rooms are cleared?"

He sent up a quick prayer for guidance and patience. She was so stubborn. Didn't she understand she and the baby needed to get to safety? Who was he kidding? When it came to Eden his judgment was skewed.

"We'll do it together," he said, deciding to compromise. "You will not leave my side." Maybe this was better—he could keep an eye on her and keep her safe.

"I can live with that condition." She marched past him to enter the exam rooms. He followed. They checked the rooms, the supply closet and the employee lounge and offices to make sure no one was left behind before they headed out into the hall. The sound of fire engines arriving on the scene bolstered Zach's confidence.

A stream of people from the other medical offices on the floor hurried toward the stairwell. The elevators were locked open, which was standard protocol when a fire alarm was pulled. Side by side, Zach and Eden, with Amber at their heels, evacuated each office on the floor before heading down the staircase to do the same on the next three floors. Satisfied the building was empty, Zach led Eden down the first-floor hallway.

"Strange," Eden muttered. "I didn't smell smoke. Did you?"

"No." Needing to get Eden to safety, he applied a slight pressure to her hip to get her moving toward the exit.

There'd been no smoke or evidence of a fire. Unease slithered across the nape of Zach's neck. Was it a false alarm? Had the killer been in the building and pulled the alarm, hoping to grab Eden while Zach was distracted with leading everyone out?

Caution tripped down Zach's spine as he reached for the side exit door.

Amber spun around with a growl.

A man wearing a black balaclava and mirrored sunglasses, and holding a gun, rushed out of the supply closet they'd just passed and grabbed Eden by the arm.

Was this the same man who'd broken into their home?

Zach reached for his weapon.

The man waved the gun at Amber and Zach. "Don't do it. Call off your dog." The man's voice was rough and low.

Zach raised his hand. Terror and rage warred within him. He needed to play this carefully so that Eden and their child weren't harmed. "Heel."

Amber obeyed the command, but the dog continued to growl, the menacing sound bouncing off the walls.

"There's nowhere for you to go," Zach said. He took a step forward.

"Stop," the assailant bit out. The barrel of his gun was aimed at Amber's head. "Take one more move and I'll shoot the dog."

"No, please," Eden said. Her panicked gaze met Zach's.

He wanted to reassure her but at the moment, he wasn't sure how they were going to survive the situation.

Tugging Eden with him, the killer backed up toward the end of the hallway where it made a T. "She's coming with me. And if you follow, she dies."

Zach didn't trust that the man didn't intend to kill Eden either way. But he had to keep his cool.

Just as the killer and Eden reached the end of the hall his gun still aimed at Amber, Eden elbowed the man in the gut and stomped on his foot.

Reacting quickly, Zach drew his weapon and shouted, "Down!"

Eden dropped to the ground.

Zach fired off a shot.

The killer lunged out of view, barely dodging the bullet aimed at his heart.

Pumped with adrenaline, Zach and Amber raced down the hall to Eden's side. Amber whined, clearly wanting to chase after the killer but Zach wouldn't take the chance the man would shoot her. "Stay," he told the dog. He gathered Eden close. "You okay?"

Her body shook but her gaze was clear. "Yes. I did good, right?"

Hearing the assailant's retreating footfalls as the man ran farther into the building, Zach hugged her. "You did real good."

He called in the situation and was assured police were already en route.

Keeping Eden close with an arm around her waist, he helped her to her feet and then with his fingers splayed over her hip led her quickly to the exit. He shielded his eyes with his free hand against the glare of sunlight reflecting off of two fire engines. Firemen corralled the building's inhabitants a safe distance away. Several firemen entered the building through the main entrance.

Zach waved to the fire chief to gain his attention and called out, "False alarm."

Sam rushed to their side. "What's happening?"

Giving him a recap of the events and why they were at the clinic, Zach finished with, "That was a close call. Too close."

Sam clapped him on the back. "Thank God all four of you are safe. Congratulations on your impending parenthood. I'll make sure the others search the building and crowd for the man you described. But I'm sure he'll ditch the mask." He gestured to where his cruiser was parked at the curb. "Slide in. I'll get you out of here."

"Thank you." Eden took a step.

But Zach held her close. "We move together."

She nodded. Her jaw was firm with determination. Respect and admiration for this woman flooded through Zach's veins. She was tough. Stronger than he'd ever given her credit for. On some level he knew that was one of many reasons he'd been drawn to her.

They moved rapidly to Sam's vehicle and slid into the back passenger compartment. Amber jumped in, also.

After Sam gave orders for the other sheriff's deputies to search for the assailant, he jumped into the driver's seat. They took off in a roar. Zach remained curled around Eden on the off chance that the killer managed to escape the building and decided to take a shot at them.

"Do you think he knows why we were there?" Eden asked, her voice shaky.

"I don't see how. There's more than obstetrics on that floor," he said.

Within moments, they were at the sheriff's station and parked in the back parking lot. Sam hurried them inside.

Once they were safely inside the building, Zach and Eden both gave Sam their statement, Zach handed his gun over as was protocol after firing his weapon for inspection, then headed to Zach's office. Amber drank a large bowl of water before settling on her bed.

Eden flopped down in one of the armchairs facing Zach's mahogany desktop. He sat in his captain's chair, breathing deeply to calm his racing heart.

"Well, that was—" Eden began. She shook her head. "I don't know what that was. Alarming. Terrifying. He's not going to stop, is he?"

Gut twisting at the despair threading through her tone, he said, "We will find him."

Her lips pressed together, then she sighed. "First, you have to identify him."

Zach grunted. He could only pray that they found shell casings with the perpetrator's fingerprints.

"I'm sorry I put you in that situation," she said softly.

"This is not your fault, Eden," he quickly assured her, hating that she'd take on any guilt for the situation. "This maniac, whoever he is, doesn't realize you can't identify him."

Eden cocked her head. "I wish I remembered more about him."

The thought gave Zach pause. What if she could remember more about the perpetrator? "Would you be willing to sit with a forensic artist?"

Eden sat up straight. "Yes. If you think it will help."

"I do." His cell phone rang. The caller ID came up as Lucy Lopez's task force number. "Lucy, everything okay?"

"Just wanted to update you on the Dakota Gun Task Force case and my investigation into the gunrunner who'd been found dead along with ex-con Petey Pawners," she said. "Jared Olin's ex-girlfriend just rescheduled our interview. She's retained counsel."

Zach gritted his teeth. Of course, the woman was entitled to a lawyer, but getting anything useful out of her now would prove more problematic. Mostly because they suspected anything she had to say would be self-incriminating. "I'll update Daniel and we can talk about making a call to the

Keystone prosecutor to see what kind of deal we can put on the table," Zach told Lucy.

"That would be helpful," Lucy said. "Do you know when you'll get back to your home?"

"Not sure," he said. "I'll be touching base with the fire chief soon." He explained what had happened at the medical clinic.

"Whoa. That's not good. Is there anything I can do to help?"

"Actually, there is something. You wouldn't happen to have the name and number of a forensic artist who could come here and meet with Eden?" The sheriff's department didn't have one on staff. Zach could reach out to nearby local law enforcement agencies but that would take time. If Lucy had a ready resource that would expedite things.

"I do, in fact." Lucy gave him the contact information for a forensic artist named Isabella Whitman. "She's freelance and travels to wherever she's needed."

"I appreciate this." After hanging up with Lucy, Zach put in a call to Isabella. She agreed to come to Keystone and meet with Eden to see if she could get a composite drawing of the man who murdered Lindsay Nash and attacked Eden.

That afternoon Eden paced the Sheriff's Department's employee lounge as she waited for the forensic artist to arrive. Nervous energy made

Eden antsy. Would she be able to describe her attacker well enough to identify him?

Zach appeared in the doorway. "She's here."

Stilling her shaking limbs, Eden followed him to the conference room, a big open space with a large oval table in the middle. A blonde woman sat at the table. Art supplies and an open laptop sat waiting. The woman rose, her low ponytail swinging, as they entered into the room. She was petite with hazel eyes and a kind smile. She didn't wear a police uniform, but rather khakis, athletic shoes and a green top that matched the green hues in her eyes.

Holding out her hand, the woman said, "Hi, I'm Isabella Whitmore. You must be Eden and Zach Kelcey. Lucy has filled me in on the situation."

Heart thumping, Eden shook the woman's hand. "Nice to meet you. I've never done this…" Eden gestured to the forensic artist's accoutrements.

"No worries, I'll talk you through the process," Isabella said. She shook hands with Zach and then resumed her seat.

Feeling out of her depth, Eden turned to Zach. She wanted to ask him to stay, but yet, this was something she needed to do on her own. "I'll be okay. You don't need to stay here."

Zach gave her a tight smile before he exited the conference room.

Alone with Isabella, Eden said, "I appreciate

you coming here to Keystone. Where are you from?"

"I'm based out of Plains City, but I travel throughout the Dakotas to whichever law enforcement agency needs me."

"That must be very interesting," Eden said. "You get to visit a lot of places and meet a lot of people."

"It can be interesting and rewarding," Isabella said. "But it can also be exhausting. I don't really have roots. The apartment I share with a friend is more for staging purposes than a home."

Eden had once thought she'd planted roots with Zach. But then Zach had ripped them up like unwanted weeds with his declaration of not wanting to be a parent. The beautiful roses he'd given her on Valentine's Day had mocked her pain. She could still see the look of horror on his face when she'd brought up the idea of starting a family. His reaction had hurt her deeply. He'd been terse and irritable after that for weeks, making her feel as if she'd done something wrong.

Now Eden was going to have to replant herself and make roots for her and her child without Zach. Sadness filled her chest to think that Zach would not be a full-time part of their lives. They would be forever linked, but it wasn't going to be how she'd envisioned her life.

For over an hour, Isabella asked questions about the attacker as she sketched, her charcoal pencil moving smoothly over the paper. She'd explained that once she had the image done by hand she would scan it into her computer for more tweaking, if needed. Isabella's questions forced Eden to dredge up the memory of the man who'd killed Lindsay and then attacked her multiple times. Eden knew this was necessary and wanted this man caught, but reliving those moments was torment.

Zach appeared in the doorway, his brow furrowed and his eyes grim. She could tell he was agitated.

Panic revved in her chest. "What's happened?"

"Reports of a child abduction."

Her stomach sank and worry for the child filled her. "You and Amber are going, correct?"

For a second his hesitation confused her, then she realized he was afraid to leave her. His protectiveness touched her heart. "I'll be fine here."

Doubts clouded his gaze.

"I have nowhere else to be," Isabella offered. "I'll stay. She'll be safe here."

His expression eased with relief. "Thank you. I'll be back as soon as possible."

"Godspeed," Eden said, as she had every time in the past year when he'd set off on a search and rescue with Amber.

With a quick nod, he left.

It was hard to concentrate knowing a young life was endangered.

Please, Lord, let Zach find the child. Let this have a good outcome.

Because she was safe within the walls of the police station, would the person who wanted to harm her transfer his deadly intent onto Zach while he was in the wilderness?

NINE

Zach arrived at the trailhead to one of the many hiking paths swathed through the Black Hills National Forest. This particular one was just outside of a town called Deadwood, South Dakota. The afternoon sun was high and warm. Search teams had already started forming, and an initial planning point had been established. He let Amber out of her compartment and hooked her into a tracking harness.

With her at his side, they jogged over to the incident command center. There were several deputy sheriffs from Lawrence County, as well as the neighboring counties, including Pennington County. They stood in a cluster around a makeshift command post beneath a white tent, focused on a table where a map of the Black Hills National Forest was spread out.

As Zach approached, Sam broke away and met him. "Glad you're here. We're about to start the search."

"When was the PLS?" Zach asked, referring to the point last seen of the missing child.

"Two hours ago. The mother," Sam said, gesturing toward a woman who stood off to the side, flanked by two patrol officers, "Barbara Davis, claims her ex-husband, Ron Davis, showed up drunk at her house in Deadwood. She has a restraining order against him. He kicked open the front door when she refused to allow him in. He took their six-year-old daughter, Lexi."

Wincing, Zach could imagine the mother's upset. When his own sister had gone missing, the first assumption had been an abduction. He'd feared the worst. Even back then the statistics were high for missing children. The majority of child abductions were perpetrated by non-custodial parents. But stranger abductions were increasing all the time. And gaining more news coverage. Those cases were the most heartbreaking. And another reason why Zach hadn't wanted to contemplate bringing a child into the world.

But that point was moot now. He and Eden were having a child. Zach would do everything in his power to keep his child from becoming a statistic. The thought sent a fresh wave of trepidation crashing through him. Was he capable of being a good parent?

Refocusing, he asked, "Why does the mother think the father brought Lexi to the forest?"

Sam swiveled and pointed to a large off-road

truck with fat tires parked haphazardly near the trailhead entrance. "The ex-husband's. A local park ranger, in the middle of giving the vehicle a ticket, ran the plates, saw the Amber Alert and now we're here. The wife says her ex-husband likes to go boondocking in the forest. Something she has not allowed him to do with their daughter."

Boondocking, or dry camping, as some called it, was camping without any facilities. A person who was prepared to boondock in the forest could hike in deep and not need to return to civilization for a very long time. Zach's gut clenched. He didn't like these kinds of rescues. How prepared was the father? Would he hurt the child? Was this abduction some sort of revenge on the mother? Zach sent up a prayer that the father wouldn't hurt his child. Anxiety twisted in his chest. For a moment, he was transported back to that day when Caron disappeared. The panic that she'd be hurt or taken permanently away from her family had lodged a thick knife-like pain in his heart.

She had suffered an injury before she was found. And it was all Zach's fault as his parents were quick to tell him over and over again. They never stopped condemning him for the damage done to his sister's leg by the horse that had stomped on it.

Shaking off the memory, Zach said, "I need

an article of clothing or something for Amber to sniff, then we can get to work."

"Come with me." Sam led Zach past the sobbing woman to the truck. He opened the front door and pointed inside. "Will that suffice?"

Zach peered around Sam to see a child's pink backpack lying on the seat. Such a sweet symbol of innocence. Much like the one found with his sister. She'd packed her backpack to go on an adventure. But this child hadn't gone of her own free will. "That will do." Instead of contaminating the scent, Zach gestured to the truck, and the black Lab easily jumped to the seat. "Sniff."

Amber took a long sniff at the backpack and the headrest, where their suspect would no doubt have the strongest scent because of the oils in his hair.

Zach gestured for Amber to jump out of the truck. The dog lifted her black nose in the air. Her ears twitched and her slim black tail wagged. Amber lunged, wanting to start her tracking. But Zach held on to the tracking harness with the long lead, tugged her back and then released a bit of tension, creating more excitement and energy. The more eager Amber was to search, the more focused she'd be. Zach wanted her engaged and raring to go. A child's life hung in the balance.

Back when Caron went missing, if the search and rescue team hadn't deployed a bloodhound to track her, she might have been gone for a lot longer.

Zach reached back into the cab of the truck and grabbed the backpack. He quickly unzipped it and peeked inside. Spotting what he needed, he grabbed a pink scrunchie with little smiling faces on it. He waved the hair tie in front of Amber's nose, letting her take a deep sniff. Then he stuffed the elastic silk-encased band into his pocket.

"We have a direction?" It was always helpful if he could cast Amber in the way they needed to go. But the scent would take them where it took them.

Sam shook his head. "My guess is they started up the official trail before veering off into the woods. I'm coming with you. Let me gear up."

While Sam grabbed supplies from the trunk of his car, Zach put extra water bottles in his utility belt and a couple of protein bars that he and Amber could consume if needed.

Sam jogged to them with a backpack slung over his shoulders. "Let's go."

"Find!" Zach gave Amber the release word.

The dog took off up the trail and soon was at the end of the tether. Zach and Sam ran behind her. For a good half hour, they followed the official park trail at a fast clip until Amber skidded to a stop. Her nose twitched, and her head swung side to side before she made a sharp left and bound into the forest.

The going was rough as they traversed deep

into the wild sections of the national forest. Brambles and thick underbrush scratched at their clothing.

But Amber's pace didn't lessen. With her nose to the ground, she kept moving, jumping easily over fallen limbs or scrabbling over boulders. Zach was glad for the thirty-three feet of cotton tracking line that allowed Amber some maneuverability and him the means to keep up.

Occasionally, Amber would lift her snout and hop as if she caught the scent again. When she had a strong scent to follow it made things easier. Zach prayed for the little girl's safety. Did she understand what was happening? Was she scared? Was the father hurting her?

Obsessive thoughts reached through his mind, shifting quickly to his family. What if it was Eden or the baby lost in these woods? What if someone took them away? What if someone had taken his sister? The possibilities scored him to the quick.

Thankfully, Caron hadn't been abducted. Instead, he'd shirked his responsibility and allowed her to wander off where she'd been injured. He carried the guilt squarely on his shoulders. And his parents never failed to remind him of the way his sister's life had been impacted by his actions.

Zach knew the heartache Barbara Davis was going through.

"Trust God," Sam said.

The words jolted through Zach's thoughts.

"What if we're too late?" Zach said. "What if he does something to the little girl?"

Shifting the backpack slightly as they moved, Sam said, "How many of these rescues have you and Amber completed?"

Zach didn't hesitate. He knew each and every one. They were like a slash crossed his heart. "Twenty-two. This is twenty-three."

"And how many of those have ended poorly?"

Zach knew where he was going with this line of questioning as they jogged along behind Amber, who continued through the thick forest. "Only two."

"That's right. Two. Neither of which had anything to do with you. In both instances, the child was deceased long before you were ever called to the scene."

Though Zach knew what Sam said was true, it didn't make those losses any easier. In each case there existed an *if*.

If he'd been called in sooner. If evil people didn't exist in the world. If God didn't let bad things happen to innocent children.

Zach shoved a branch out of his way with more force than necessary.

"Dude, what's going on in that head of yours?" Sam said.

Guilt flooded his system for blaming God for the actions of humans. "I guess the realization that I'm becoming a father has me all kinds of screwed up inside."

"That's fear talking," Sam said. "Fear's whole purpose is to create chaos, despair and unhappiness. Don't let it control you."

"I can't seem to shake it," Zach said.

Amber stopped and then doubled back a few paces. Zach and Sam caught up to her. Zach brought out the hair tie again and held it out for Amber to sniff.

She went still. Her head swiveled and her namesake amber-colored eyes peered into the darkening forest to the right. She let out a bark and bounded off in a new direction.

Keeping up took all of Zach's focus as he and Sam followed Amber deeper and deeper into the woods. Shadows grew as the sun began its descent. The air cooled beneath the canopy of tree limbs dense with foliage.

"I think we're headed toward Mount Roosevelt Friendship Tower," Sam said.

"We're circling back toward town?" Zach couldn't get his bearings. He was too focused on Amber and her body language. Her ears were up, her movements purposeful and her stride sure. She was tracking the child.

"Seems like it. The suspect intends to make his way back to Deadwood and then disappear with his daughter," Sam said.

They reached a point where the ground appeared to be disturbed. As if there had been a struggle. Zach reeled Amber in and brought her to his side as he crouched. Using his flashlight, he and Sam looked closely at the dirt. He could make out the faint impressions of a man's shoe. And a smaller print that had to belong to Lexi.

Amber's nose twitched. She pulled at the lead, her body turning in one direction and then the other as if she'd picked up two scents. Had the little girl managed to break away from her father?

Zach pulled out the scrunchie and let Amber take another whiff. "Find."

Amber didn't hesitate. She took off to the left. The terrain climbed. Night fell. The sounds of the forest were quiet as if sensing intruders.

When they reached the summit, breaking through the tree line, they came out to the towering stone edifice. The fire watchtower had been erected as a dedication to President Theodore Roosevelt back in 1919 by the then Deadwood sheriff, Seth Bullock. For years, the monolith had stood empty and decayed, forgotten. But over the years, conservationists revamped the lookout as a tourist destination for hikers. Though there was no ranger on staff here, the park rangers did occasionally come and check on the structure.

Amber pulled toward the stairs leading to the open entryway cut into the side of the stone wall. Zach exchanged a glance with Sam, though the ambient light of the moon hardly allowed visibility. Zach kept his free hand on his holstered weapon as he and Sam followed Amber into the dark interior.

The bottom of the tower was empty. A musty coldness seeped through Zach's uniform. Amber ignored the dark crevices and instead pulled toward the curving stone stairs leading up to the top of the watchtower. Zach said a prayer that they would find the child unharmed.

When they came out at the landing, Amber rushed forward toward a shadowed curve far from the two watchtower windows. Zach flipped on his flashlight. Sam did the same. Light illumined the room and revealed a child on the floor, curled over her knees with her head down, apparently trying to make herself as small as possible.

Zach almost went to his knees with relief. This was the part he lived for. Bringing home the missing. Finding redemption for others when he couldn't find redemption for himself. Even twenty-one successful search and rescue missions later, he couldn't seem to forgive himself for his sister going missing on his watch.

He used the radio on his uniform to call in that they'd found the child unharmed. He gave dispatch their location. The command center would pack up and head to the trailhead leading to the Friendship Tower.

Amber sniffed the child and then sat beside the little girl with her tongue lolling to the side.

"You did well," Zach said and pulled out a tug toy. Amber moved to grab the toy.

Sam approached the child, hands up, showing he meant no harm.

"Lexi, your mom sent us," he said gently.

The little girl lifted her tear-streaked face and blinked at them. Dirt smeared her face. Her jeans were ripped at one knee and leaves stuck out of her dark hair. "Mama?"

At the sound of the little girl's voice, Amber dropped the tug toy and trotted back to the child, pushing her way past Sam to allow the child to hug her neck.

"Do you know where your father went?" Sam asked gently.

The little girl shook her head violently and buried her face into Amber's fur.

"Do you know where he was taking you?"

"He said far away where Mommy would never find me," she said with a sob. "I didn't want to go."

Anger surfaced within Zach as it always did when a child was abducted.

Now that he was going to be a father, he understood even more how devastating the situation could be for the parent. How devastating it would be for him if... He cut off the thought. "We should get her back to her mom."

"Lexi, I'm going to pick you up, okay?" Sam asked.

"Okay." Lexi released her hold on Amber and allowed Sam to lift her into his arms.

Zach reeled Amber back in and headed her down the stairs first. Amber would alert if the father had doubled back and was waiting for them outside. Using caution, Zach stepped out of the watchtower and assessed the threat level. When Amber didn't alert, Zach said, "Clear."

Sam exited the tower with Lexi in his arms. Together, they made their way down the trail leading to the entrance. Lights lit up the night sky. People gathered around. An ambulance stood waiting nearby. And reporters were held back by patrol officers.

"Lexi!"

"Mama." The little girl scrambled out of Sam's arms and ran to her mother.

Zach took a beat to watch the happy reunion. Then he realized he was also on camera as reporters surged forward. Bright lights stung his eyes and that of Amber. She turned so that her back was to the lights and stared up at him as she had been trained.

"Deputy Kelcey, is it true the K-9 found the child?" a reporter Zach recognized from the local television station called out. He covered most of the search and rescue cases in the area.

Another asked, "Was the little girl found inside the Mount Roosevelt Friendship Tower?"

And another shouted, "Did you find the father?"

The incident command chief, the current Lawrence County sheriff, stepped in front of the cameras. "I will give you all a statement."

Leaving the sheriff to deal with the media, Zach and Amber slipped away and walked over to the little girl and her mom. He held out the pink scrunchie. "You might want to save this."

The mother took the scrunchie and Zach's hand. Tears streamed down her face. "I don't know how to thank you both."

"Just doing our job, ma'am," Zach said.

"Thank you for finding me," the little girl said. Though her gaze was on Amber.

Catching Sam's eye, Zach excused himself and hurried to his friend's side.

"We have a report of Ron Davis boarding a bus," Sam said.

"Mr. Davis must have heard us approaching and realized his daughter would slow him down so he opted to ditch her and make his way to the bus depot to try to escape," Zach said.

Sam nodded. "Officers are en route to intercept. He'll be in custody by daybreak."

Satisfied with a good ending to this search and rescue, Zach hurried away from the scene, anxious to get back to his wife and child. He didn't know how much longer he would be able to claim them both. But for now, they were his, and he would do everything in his power to protect them.

On the television in the Sheriff's Department employee lounge, the news showed the dramatic rescue of the missing little girl. Seeing Zach, Amber and Sam, who carried the child, emerge from the darkness and into the light had Eden folding her hands and pressing them to her lips in gratitude that her prayers for a safe return of the child had been answered.

Feeling as if a weight had lifted off her shoulders, Eden smiled at Isabella. "He'll be back soon."

"They are impressive," the other woman said.

Indeed, they were. "I appreciate you staying here with me. But really, you should head home. Your job is done. I'll be fine. I know Zach and Sam will be eager to see the composite sketch you did."

"I'll wait," Isabella replied. "That way I can hand it over directly. And if there are any issues with loading it into the national crime databases, I'll be here to make any adjustments."

"I'm sure they'd appreciate your due diligence." After making herself another cup of herbal tea, Eden settled on the lounge's leather couch to wait for Zach and Amber to return so they could go back to the rental house. She wanted to crawl into bed and sleep for a week.

The past few hours had been nerve-racking as they'd waited to learn the outcome of the rescue. Now that she knew the child was safe and Zach and Amber were safe, the adrenaline from the day's events ebbed away, leaving her groggy. She'd just close her eyes for a moment.

She felt a gentle hand on her shoulder.

"Eden."

Blinking away the fog of sleep, Eden stared up at her husband. He looked tired, with dark circles under his eyes and dirt smearing his uniform. Her traitorous heart leaped with joy. She tempered it with a quick check. No. She was glad he'd returned safe and sound because she was a good person, not because she was still in love with him. How could she be when he'd hurt her so badly by trying to deny her the one thing she'd wanted most?

Yet, she carried a child, his child, just as she'd dreamed.

She sat up. "We saw you on the news. You and Amber are heroes."

Zach helped her to her feet. "Today was a win. Are you ready to go?"

"Yes, please." She glanced around but they were alone. "Where's Isabella?"

"She left. She said to tell you that you did well," Zach replied and led her out the door to his waiting vehicle.

They arrived back at the rental in no time.

Before she headed down the hall to the bedroom, he said, "I heard from the fire chief. He cleared the house. We can go over tomorrow to grab some things."

"We can move back in?"

"No. Though there was minimal water and smoke damage to the body of the house, the garage needs to be torn down and rebuilt. The fire chief strongly suggests we wait to inhabit the home until after the repairs."

She was too tired to stress about the house tonight. "Thank you for letting me know." She hesitated, part of her wanting to slip into his embrace and another part wanting to pummel him for destroying their marriage. Tears pricked her eyes. "Good night, Zach."

Tomorrow she would take control back of her life, whether her husband liked it or not.

TEN

The next morning, Zach and Amber waited for Eden in the living room of the house they'd once shared. She was packing a bag of her things so that they could return to the rental cottage. She'd insisted as soon they'd eaten breakfast on coming over since the fire chief had given permission to enter.

The arson investigators so far had concurred with Zach's assessment. The burning of the garage had been arson. Someone, presumably Lindsay Nash's killer, had left an open canister of acetone near the outside back corner of the garage. They had stuffed a rag into the can and then lit the rag on fire to give the suspect enough time to run away before the acetone exploded.

Eden walked out of the primary suite with a suitcase in hand.

Zach tilted his head, taking in her park ranger uniform. "What gives?"

"I've been thinking and praying all night," Eden said. "There's no reason I can't be at the park working in the office with my boss so that you can go do your job."

Zach made a scoffing sound in his throat.

Eden raised an eyebrow.

"The doctor said rest would be good for you," Zach reminded her. "Rest and work are exact opposites of each other."

"She also said I could work," she said. "Whether I'm sitting around watching TV at the rental or sitting at a desk answering phones, both are sedentary and restful. I'd rather be useful than useless. I'll be safe in the park offices behind locked doors."

A trait he'd always appreciated in her but now found frustrating. Being idle was not something Eden did well. Even on their weekends when they both had the day off, while he'd wanted to sleep in or relax in the backyard with a book, she'd found chores to do. And when those were done, she would move on to gardening or some craft project. He'd never minded her constant activity as long as they were together. "I can't do my job from the park."

"You can't do your job from the rental house, either," she pointed out.

He hated the truth in her words. "My boss has given me some time to deal with our situation."

Eden narrowed her gaze. "Dealing with our situation would be working toward finding Lindsay Nash's murderer. That should be your top priority. And you can't do that while babysitting me inside the rental house."

He opened his mouth to argue, though what exactly he could say to her logic he wasn't quite sure, but she stalled him with a hand up.

"Before you launch into some kind of diatribe," Eden said. "Let me remind you my boss, Matt Acosta, is a former army ranger. He will be with me the whole time. I've already talked to him."

"I don't diatribe," Zach said.

"Yeah, actually you do," Eden said as she walked past him. "It's how you process, Zach."

Was it? He'd never really thought that through. He gave himself a mental shake. It didn't matter.

"Eden, be reasonable," Zach said. "I—"

"I am being reasonable. You need to get out there and find the killer." She moved closer so that they were standing nearly toe-to-toe.

Eden put her hand on his chest. Beneath the fresh Pennington sheriff's deputy uniform he'd put on this morning, his heart rate sped up. As if it hadn't already been racing like a thoroughbred right out of the gate. Why did she have this effect on him? No other woman had ever been able to get him to bend to their will with just a look or touch.

Was what she was proposing that preposterous? Zach trusted Matt and knew the older gentleman could handle himself and anyone who tried to get to Eden and their baby. But it was Zach's job to protect her. However, it was also his job to find the killer. And to find the weapons trafficking organization that was running rampant through the Dakotas.

Tension ratcheted through his muscles, tightening them until he thought he might pop a vein.

"Let me check in with Sam and Matt and then I will make a decision," he told Eden. Hoping that one of them could talk some sense into her.

She patted his chest. "It's cute that you think you have any say in this."

He growled as she picked up her suitcase and walked out the door.

Zach released a pent-up breath of frustration and anxiety that came out almost like a moan. Amber sat at his feet and cocked her head. "Don't judge me. Happy wife, happy life, right?"

Locking up behind them, he realized that clichéd saying wasn't true in their situation. Soon Eden would not be his wife. Soon they would be only connected through a child. A connection that would forever bind them together. Just as the commitment they'd made to each other should.

A deep ache had him rubbing the spot over his heart.

After putting Amber in her compartment, Zach walked around to the driver's side door but hesitated before climbing into the vehicle. He lifted up a prayer. "Lord, I don't want to disappoint you. I don't want to go against your will. But we need some mighty intervention here. Some guidance. Amen."

Just how God would orchestrate a satisfying conclusion to the situation Zach didn't know. But he supposed that's what walking out in faith meant. Not knowing how the future would unfold but trusting in God's plan.

What choice did Zach have?

As Eden settled at a workstation inside the ranger station located near the entrance of Mount Rushmore, she knew without a doubt Zach, standing next to her desk, wasn't happy. He did not like this arrangement. Leaving her in the care of her boss wasn't Zach's preference, but she had agency enough to dictate how her life would go. She didn't need her husband—well, soon-to-be ex-husband—telling her what to do. She would be safe here with her boss, a former army ranger, on guard, allowing Zach to go back to work. She needed space from him to think, to process. They were having a baby!

A mix of elation, anxiety and sorrow balled in her gut. She was elated to be pregnant, to be creating a child. A child she would love beyond measure. However, the uncertainty of the future and the threat to her life caused apprehension to take root. But it was the sorrow of her marriage dissolving that made her want to cry.

"It's not too late to change your mind," Zach said. "I can stay."

The worry in his eyes both touched and irritated her. She was tempted to keep him close, yet she needed to push him away. "Just go already," she said, cringing at the sharpness of her words. She tempered her tone by adding, "Matt has already given you assurances." She nodded toward her boss, sitting at his own desk and doing a terrible job of pretending not to be listening. "No one can get in the locked door without him letting them in. I can watch the monitors to see if anyone who looks like Lindsay's killer is in the park."

Though his tight expression conveyed he was less than pleased, Zach nodded and left the ranger station.

"You're being a little hard on him," Matt said without looking up from his computer.

Eden sighed with a bit of guilt and remorse but more with exasperation. The turmoil going on inside of her was tedious and exhausting. Maybe it was the flux of hormones from the pregnancy. Tears pricked the backs of her eyes, and she blinked them away. Had to be the hormones. "I don't mean to be. I just don't know how to navigate this situation."

She thought back to last Thanksgiving when he'd been struggling with the decision to go to his parents for the holiday dinner. He'd known it was the right thing to do, but he hadn't wanted to go.

Eden didn't understand all the nuances of Zach's relationship with his father and mother, but they were still his parents and she had to push to make him go because she worried he'd regret not going.

The evening had been pleasurable despite an undercurrent of tension that ran through the family, and it had only grown more intense when his sister, Caron, had arrived with her husband and two boys. Eden had loved getting on the floor and playing with the four-year-old and six-year-old.

She had caught Zach watching them with a pained expression that had left her both confused and worried. She'd sensed tension between him and his parents, but his sister had always been warm and loving toward her big brother. Did his strained relationship with his parents have anything to do with his aversion to having children? Had that been why he seemed uncomfortable when she'd played with his nephews?

Now that she thought back on their year-long marriage, there were so many times when it came to his family that he hedged or redirected the conversation away to something else. As if he hadn't wanted to bring them into their relationship. But they were his family. A part of him. She'd always told herself he would open up eventually. They had a lifetime to get to know each other.

She could almost hear the echo of her father's admonishment of how impulsive the decision was to marry a man after only two months of knowing him.

Well, she and Zach had proceeded. And now she was pregnant. She decided she would need to get to know this man who was going to be sharing the responsibility of the child she carried. But that would have to wait until Lindsay's killer was brought to justice.

"Okay, boss, what tasks can I jump on?" Keeping busy was the only way to keep her mind from worry.

Zach met with Lucy at the Pennington County Sheriff's Department, doing his best to leave his worry about Eden closed up in the small office of the rangers' station. Leaving Amber on her bed at his desk, he secured an interview room for Jared Olin's ex-girlfriend Desiree Weiner and her legal counsel. After a lengthy discussion with the local prosecutor, Zach had secured an immunity deal dependent on the information Desiree gave them.

Zach paced outside the interview room as they waited for Desiree and her lawyer.

"What has you so worked up?" Lucy asked from her place on a bench lining the hallway. Piper lay at her feet.

"I don't like being away from Eden," he told her. So much for boxing up his worry about his wife.

"You trust her boss, don't you?"

"I do." Because he did. But Zach couldn't quite put his finger on what was running through his veins. It wasn't distrust of Matt or the man's ability to protect Eden. She would be safe ensconced inside the ranger station's locked offices. It was just this general sense of anxiety that was crawling through him. Because of the danger? Or because of the baby? He decided that talking to the pastor of their church would be a good idea.

Lucy stood, prompting Piper to stand and stretch. "Here we go."

Zach turned to find a woman with long dark hair, dressed in pleated linen slacks, heeled shoes, and a red blouse, walking toward them with a very well-dressed man at her side. The red power tie and tailored navy suit screamed a man out to influence.

"Deputy Kelcey?" the man said as he and the woman stopped in front of Zach and Lucy.

"I am," Zach said. "Desiree Weiner?"

She blinked at him before turning her gaze to the man.

"Yes, this is Desiree," the man stated. "I am her lawyer, Scott Tenant."

This was going to be a long interview if Desiree was going to look to Scott to answer their questions.

"This way, please," Lucy said, opening the door to the interview room. She held Piper at her side.

Desiree and Scott walked into the interview

room and paused near the table, where two sets of chairs were positioned opposite each other on either side of it.

Zach shared a curious glance with Lucy. She appeared to be wondering the same thing he was. How could Desiree afford such a high-priced lawyer?

The thrum of anticipation coursed through Zach. Could Desiree be the break in the trafficking ring they were hoping for?

"Have a seat," Lucy said, indicating the two chairs on the opposite side of the table from where she stood.

Once everyone was seated, Zach said, "As my colleague explained, we have questions regarding Jared Olin. We understand you were his girlfriend."

Desiree looked to Scott, who gave a slight nod.

"Ex-girlfriend," Desiree said. "I dumped Jared a while back."

"Can you explain why?" Lucy asked.

Once again, Desiree looked to Scott for approval before answering the question. She said, "He was getting involved in criminal activity that I was uncomfortable with. I'm sorry he's dead. But he brought it on himself."

"Can you expound on the criminal activity?" Zach probed.

"No, I can't. I didn't want to know so I didn't ask."

Reining in his frustration, Zach asked, "Do you know the names of any of Jared Olin's associates? Did he ever mention anyone in particular?"

After seeking approval from Scott, who nodded his permission, Desiree said, "He mentioned someone by the name of Brandon a few times. I got the sense he admired the guy. Wanted to be like him." She rolled her dark eyes. "Jared had a habit of finding the latest, greatest guru to follow. Usually into some predicament that would lead to trouble."

Brandon was a name they had not heard in relation to the trafficking ring. Was Brandon somehow involved? Is that how Jared got involved? "Did you ever meet Brandon?"

"Go ahead and show them," Scott said, prompting Desiree to take her phone from the pocket of her jacket.

"I never met the guy," Desiree said, "but Jared sent me a photo of the two of them a several months ago. I think he was trying to get back together. I complained often he was so secretive and never allowed me to have a picture of him. He sent this picture with this guy in front of our lunch spot. I guess he was thinking if I saw his face, I'd realize I missed him." She held up the image on the phone.

Perking up at the potential clue, Zach wanted to enlarge the picture to better see the man's features. "Can you text it to me?"

He gave her his cell phone number, and a moment later his phone dinged and the picture popped up on the screen. He and Lucy looked at the photo and then at each other. Whoa. The photo was taken in front of the Plains City Pizzeria. The very place where West Cole saw Jared Olin loading shipments of guns in the back of a van along with Petey Pawners just an hour before both men were gun downed at a gas station.

"That's all I know. I don't want to talk anymore." Desiree stood.

Her lawyer was slower to rise. "If you have any more questions for my client, you may contact me." He laid down a business card on the interview room table. Then he escorted his client out.

"I'm going to forward this photo to Cheyenne to see what information she can find out about this Brandon guy."

Lucy's phone dinged. "Hey, there's a task force video call we need to jump on."

"We'll do it at my desk." Feeling energized because they finally had a lead, Zach led Lucy through the Pennington County Sheriff's Department to his desk in the back corner. Amber, who had been resting on her bed, lifted her head as they approached. Piper moved to sniff Amber in greeting then the two dogs settled down. Lucy pulled a vacant chair over to the side of Zach's desk while he fired up his desktop computer and opened up the video chat link. The screen populated. The task force was comprised of law enforcement professionals from across the Dakotas, so most of them were spread out, working from their home bases and traveling as necessary. Video meetings enabled the team to get together and share progress on the case.

The Dakota Gun Task Force leader, Daniel Slater, brought the meeting to order. "It's good to see you all. Zach, are you any closer to catching the park ranger's killer?"

"The Sheriff's Department investigator is following up right now, including the results of a forensic sketch. I'll check in with him once we're done here."

"And the fire at your house and the trouble at the medical center? Is everybody okay?"

"Yes, we're fine. The arson was contained to the garage and Eden was kept safe at the medical building."

Zach glanced at Lucy, giving her a nod to speak up.

"Daniel, Zach and I just finished interviewing Jared Olin's ex-girlfriend. She gave us a name that we've passed on to Cheyenne."

"Good work, you two," Daniel said. "Hopefully the lead will provide useful information, because at the moment we are at a standstill."

Zach's cell phone rang and he checked the screen. "It's Cheyenne."

"Take it," Daniel said. "We can sign off for now. Zach, keep me updated."

Zach nodded and clicked the end button for the video call as he answered the phone, putting it on speaker. "Hey, Cheyenne, I'm here with Lucy. What do you have for us?"

"I'm still working on this photo of Jared and the other guy you sent," the tech analyst said. "I'm running the image through every facial recognition software program I have access to. But I did find something else you might find interesting. In my probe into Jon Fielding, I uncovered that he signed up to do a park tour yesterday morning."

Adrenaline spiking, Zach said, "That puts him in the park at the time of Lindsay's death and when Eden was attacked."

"Exactly. I've been working with the park's security office, combing through their video surveillance feeds, but so far there are no images of Jon Fielding."

"So even though he signed up for the tour," Lucy said, "we don't know for certain he was actually in the park."

"That is correct," Cheyenne said.

"The man Eden described was blond," Zach said. "Jon could have been wearing a disguise."

"Possibly. I did look for the blond guy, too. He was careful to keep his face turned away from the cameras," Cheyenne told them. "As for Jon Fielding, there has been no other credit card charges on any of his accounts. Nor his wife's."

Zach told Cheyenne that Eden had heard from Julie Fielding and she was in a shelter.

"That makes sense then, that there would be no activity recorded on her accounts."

"Thank you, Cheyenne," Zach said. "As soon as you get any information on this Brandon character, can you let the task force know?"

"Of course." Cheyenne bid them goodbye and hung up.

His worry for Eden flared. "I think I'll head back to the park," Zach said.

"Good idea," Lucy said. "I'll take the opportunity to call home. I want to hear my little girl's voice."

Something inside of Zach throbbed with a mix of anticipation and trepidation. What would it feel like to hear his own child's voice? What would it be like to hold his baby? To feel that little body in his arms and to look into the sweet face of a newborn? Would the baby have Eden's eyes? His nose?

The questions played havoc with his mind as he hooked Amber to the leash and followed Lucy and Piper to the front door. They said goodbye and went their separate ways. Trying to gain control of his need to protect Eden, Zach focused instead on giving her practical support. Pregnant women needed to eat, right? So he stopped by thc Keystone Diner and grabbed lunch to go for him and Eden.

At the park, Zach found a spot in the employee lot next to Eden's small SUV. He and Amber made their way to the ranger's offices. Eden buzzed them in.

"I didn't expect you back until the end of the day," Eden told him as she bent to greet Amber with a scrub behind the ears and a hug. The dog's tongue lolled, clearly enjoying the attention from Eden.

Zach ignored the spurt of jealousy at the attention Amber was getting. "I was thinking you might be hungry for some lunch." He held up the bag.

A wide smile graced her pretty face and sent his heart reeling. "You read my mind."

Matt rose from his desk. "I don't suppose you brought me lunch?"

Zach winced. He should have thought about the fact Eden shared an office with a big, undoubtedly hungry guy. He shrugged apologetically. "Sorry."

The older man laughed. "No worries. Now that you're here to relive me, I'll grab something in Carver's Café." He was referring to the park's only eatery.

When they were alone, Zach brought Eden up to speed on what they'd learned about Jon Fielding.

"That's concerning," Eden said as she ate a

french fry. "When we're done with our meal, we should take a walk through the park and talk to some of the other rangers and ask if they knew who Lindsay was dating."

"I'm sure Sam has already questioned them."

"True," Eden said between bites of her ham sandwich. "But they might have remembered something since they were initially questioned. And maybe they will be more willing to open up to a fellow ranger."

He couldn't fault her logic. After they ate, they headed out into the park. Zach's senses were on high alert. The killer could be in the park. As the warm June sun and the pine-scented air swirled around them, his gaze constantly searched for a threat. They asked several of the park ranger guides, but none knew who Lindsay was dating nor if there was anyone she had a problem with who also lived in the summer dormitories.

Zach's phone rang. "It's Sam. Hopefully, he has an update for us."

He and Eden stepped to the side, away from the tourists walking the path up to the monument, and he held the phone up so they could both hear Sam when he answered.

Sam said, "Lindsay's childhood best friend said Lindsay was dating a park ranger by the name of Pat Dunbar."

Eden gasped. "He was one of the blond employees on the park's website."

"I noticed that, too," Sam said. "I've sent deputies to his house to bring him in for questioning."

"I'd like to be in on that interview," Zach said.

"I can appreciate that," Sam said. "As soon as he's brought in, I'll give you a ring," Sam promised and hung up.

"Now what?" Eden asked as they walked back toward the ranger station.

Zach shrugged. "We hope that with Pat Dunbar taken into custody, the threat to your life will end."

"And if it isn't Pat?"

He hated seeing the fear in her eyes. Acid churned in his gut. "Then this nightmare isn't over."

ELEVEN

After leaving Eden in her boss's capable hands at the park ranger station, Zach headed to the Pennington County Sheriff's Department's satellite office in downtown Keystone. The office was nestled between two tourist shops on the main strip of the low-lining, Old West-style buildings that attract visitors to their small town. In the distance, he heard the Black Hills Central Railroad 1880 Train whistle, another local attraction that took guests on a round-trip ride through the mountains from Keystone to Hill City.

He entered the building with Amber and headed straight to Sam's office. The deputy investigator stood and moved out from behind his desk as Zach and Amber stepped through the office doorway. Amber greeted the other man with a sniff, then sat with her expectant gaze trained on Zach.

"I'm glad you're here," Sam said. "They just brought Pat Dunbar in, and he's sitting in an interrogation room."

Anticipation revved in Zach's gut. "Did he come peacefully?"

"He did." Sam led the way down the hall and paused outside the interrogation room. "I'd prefer to interview him alone. He'll be more likely to talk with only one officer in the room. You two can observe from the observation room."

Sam opened the door and disappeared inside. Zach hustled Amber to the next door and entered the observation room. Amber settled on the floor at Zach's feet. Zach studied the suspect through a two-way mirror built into the wall. Pat Dunbar was a blond man with wide shoulders. He sat hunched over the table in the interrogation room's plastic chair.

"Mr. Dunbar, thank you for coming in." Sam took the seat across from Pat.

Lifting his gray eyes from the table, Pat's broad forehead wrinkled. "What is this about?"

Sam placed a notepad and a file folder on the tabletop. "Just a friendly chat."

"Friendly?" Pat scoffed. "The deputies who brought me in were not friendly. They made it seem as if I had no choice but to come here."

Opening the file folder to reveal a picture of Lindsay Nash in her ranger uniform, Sam turned the photo so that Pat could see it. "We want to talk to you about Lindsay Nash."

Zach watched Pat carefully. Grief crossed the man's face. Real? Or was it manufactured?

"I don't know what I can tell you about her death." Pat's voice broke.

"You were having a relationship with the deceased?" Sam placed his hands on the table.

Pat's eyes narrowed. Red stains infused his cheeks. "She was over twenty-one."

Zach barely contained a snort. Lindsay may have been over the legal age, but Pat Dunbar was at least twenty years her senior.

"I understand that you were supposed to meet Lindsay at the park yesterday," Sam said.

The news was a surprise to Zach.

Pat frowned. "I wasn't in the park yesterday doing a tour. And I did not see Lindsay. Our plans were for the evening. It was supposed to be her day off."

"You didn't know she was working yesterday morning?"

Pat shook his head. "She never mentioned picking up a shift."

"When was the last time you talked to Lindsay?" Sam pressed.

"The night before," Pat said.

"What did you talk about?"

Pat shrugged. "Life. About hiking sometime this month when we both had a day off."

"According to Lindsay's bunk mate, she had been acting strangely lately. Secretive. Scared even." Sam's voice took on a hard-edged tone.

Zach leaned toward the window, waiting for Pat's response.

Pat tucked in his chin. Zach couldn't say whether his jaw was square or not.

"I don't know why." Pat's voice rose. "She didn't say anything to me about being scared. But someone had it out for her. They killed her!"

"Where were you yesterday morning?" The hard note in Sam's voice echoed through the room.

Pat's eyes got round. "You think I killed her?" He shook his head. "No. No way. I don't know anything about Lindsay being scared or secretive. I didn't see her yesterday. I was conducting a guided tour outside the park when she was—" He choked up. Big fat tears welled in his eyes.

His grief appeared genuine, but Zach had seen a number of criminals who were good actors.

"Were you conducting a tour through Mount Rushmore National Memorial?" Sam asked.

"No, this was something I did on my own," Pat said. "I took a group on a five-mile hike to Horsethief Lake to a fishing hole. We were there for several hours before hiking back out. No law says I can't have a side business."

He could be innocent...but Horsethief Lake put him in the area of the murder. He was only about ten minutes away from the Presidential Trail when his girlfriend had been murdered. Could Pat have slipped out to meet Lindsay at some point and made his way back while the hiking group stopped for a break? The man clearly knew the area well and could probably move through it quickly.

Sam tapped a finger on the table. "Do you know who Lindsay was friendly with here in town?"

"Only the other park rangers, as far as I know," Pat said. "Though she was here last summer. But our paths hadn't crossed until this year."

"I need the names of the tourists you were guiding." Sam took a pen from the pocket of his uniform shirt and slid it and the notebook toward the man.

"I don't know them off the top of my head," Pat said. "I would have to email them to you from my home computer."

Sam stood. "I'll have a deputy run you home and get that list."

"I don't have time for that." Pat spread his hands wide. "I have a tour at the park."

Pat was guiding a tour so soon after his girlfriend's murder?

Strange. But maybe he was throwing himself into his work to avoid thinking about the loss. People grieved in a multitude of ways. Zach had seen many different reactions to grief, from stoic numbness to hysteria. Processing emotional trauma was a very personal experience.

"I'm sure you'll be able to manage your time," Sam said. "Tell me about Eden Kelcey?"

Zach tensed. His focus became razor-sharp on Pat.

"What about her?" Pat rose from the chair. "She's one of the regular rangers. I know her name but have never met the woman. Our paths haven't crossed."

Zach wasn't sure he believed the man, but it lined up with what Eden had said about her never having met Pat.

Sam ended the interview and escorted Pat out of the interrogation room.

Once Pat Dunbar was in the custody of a deputy, who would take him home where he could provide his alibi list, Zach and Amber met with Sam in the deputy's office. "What do you think?"

"Hard to tell." Sam moved to sit at his desk. Stacks of case files obscured the oak top. "I'll be anxious to get that list of names of those who can verify where he was at the time of Lindsay Nash's murder and Eden's attack."

So would Zach. "I think I'll head to the park. Maybe catch a tour."

After a beat, Sam said, "Tread lightly, my friend."

"Always," Zach promised as he headed out of the sheriff's station. But he couldn't shake the sense of foreboding that came over him.

Eden was deep into filing tour guide reports when the door to the office of the ranger station buzzed open. She glanced up to see her husband—her breath hitched—soon to be ex-husband walk in dressed in civilian clothes.

He was so good-looking it made her ache. Tall and slim, in dark denim and a Western-style plaid button-up shirt, Zach exuded confidence and masculinity. He had his black Stetson jammed on his head. His cowboy-booted feet echoed on the linoleum floor as he walked toward her. Her mouth went dry. Her heart thumped against her breastbone. She forced herself to look away. "I didn't expect you for another couple of hours."

"Plans change," he said, and though she wasn't looking at him, she could hear the grin in his voice.

"I'm not ready to leave." Though in all honesty her back needed a break and she was feeling just a bit queasy. Tomorrow she would remember to pack some saltine crackers and ginger ale.

"That's okay," Zach replied. "I'm going to take one of the tours with Pat Dunbar."

From his place at his desk, Matt asked, "Why with Pat?"

Eden grimaced. She hadn't told Matt about the relationship between Lindsay and Pat.

"It's come to our attention that Lindsay Nash and Pat Dunbar were having a romantic relationship," Zach said.

Matt frowned, the displeasure clear in the way his jaw firmed and his eyes hardened. "Pat should know better. I expect shenanigans from the summer interns. They always have some sort of relationship drama going on. But Pat's too old for that nonsense." Matt's eyes widened. "Do you believe Pat killed Lindsay?"

Holding her breath, Eden waited for Zach to answer.

"He's a person of interest." Zach carefully dodged the direct question.

Eden closed the file drawer and took the stack of file folders she'd been working through and set them on her desk. "I'm going with you." She turned to Matt. "If that's okay with you?"

Matt grunted and waved away her concern. "Of course."

A resigned expression crossed Zach's face. "I thought you might like to go. But I would suggest not wearing your ranger uniform. That might raise his suspicions. He claims he's never met you."

She nodded. "He's right. We've never met. And my picture on the website is from my first year here. My hair was short then and I was ten pounds heavier." She flipped back her braid. "I think I look a bit different."

"But if he's our killer, he'll recognize you and me from the attack at the house," Zach pointed out.

"And we'll be there to see his reaction and you can take him down."

"Point taken. I just would rather not put you in harm's way."

"Do you really think he'd do something with so many witnesses? If he's the one, he'll most likely take off running. Right?" She didn't wait for him to answer but headed toward the door. "Good thing I have a change of clothes in my locker."

Zach beat her to the door and put his hand on the doorknob. "I'll go with you."

She chafed at the offer. She didn't need a baby-sitter while she changed her outfit. But she didn't want to make a big deal out of the situation.

Eden, with Zach on her heels, walked out of the office and down the hall to the women's locker room. "Where's Amber?"

"I left her at the rental in her kennel," he said. "Pat would think it odd of me to bring a working dog into the park."

"True," she agreed. "Pets are allowed in limited areas, but not on a tour." At the entrance to the locker room, she held up a hand to Zach. "Let me make sure no one's in there."

"That's my job," he said, moving past her.

She snagged his elbow. "You're not going into the ladies' employee locker room."

He seemed to consider her words. He moved to the threshold of the entrance and called out, "Everybody decent in here?"

No one replied, which led Eden to believe the locker room was empty. "You can wait here."

He nodded, crossed his arms over his chest and leaned against the wall.

She pushed past Zach and headed for her locker at the end of a row. She quickly undid the lock combination and opened the long locker. She made short work of changing into a pair of khaki capris, a lightweight zip-up hoodie over a T-shirt and a pair of sneakers. She put a white athletic baseball-style hat on her head and threaded her hair through the back hole. She grabbed a pair of sunglasses from the top shelf, as well. Then she joined Zach in the hallway.

He wore sunglasses too and nodded approvingly. "You look like any other tourist." He pushed away from the wall, and they walked toward the exit. "You stay close to my side."

Thankful for the sunglasses as they stepped into the late afternoon sunshine, Eden's gaze zeroed in on the man they were looking for.

Near the visitor's kiosk, a group had assembled around a blond-haired man with broad shoulders wearing a park ranger uniform.

Pat Dunbar.

A shudder of nervous energy cascaded across her skin.

Eden studied him. Was he the man who'd attacked her? Without the big mirrored sunglasses, it was hard to tell.

She grimaced with uncertainty. She didn't want to make an accusation without evidence. "I can't be sure he's the same man who killed Lindsay and attacked me."

Beside her, Zach nodded. "Same here. I can't say he's the man I fought with. But until we can rule him out, he's a suspect. And if nothing else, he might know something." He cupped her elbow. "Let's join them."

They walked to the edge of the gathering. It had been a long time since she'd joined one of the formal tours.

"You all are in for a real treat," Pat said, his deep voice resonating through the quiet of the afternoon. "We are going to take a walk down the Avenue of Flags, which commemorates the bicentennial of the United States. From there we will head to the Sculptor's Studio, visit the Grand View Terrace and amphitheater then walk along the Presidential Trail to the Talus Terrace to see the iconic monuments up close."

The thought of standing on the platform where Lindsay had been murdered sent waves of anxiety crashing through Eden. As if sensing her upset, Zach put his arm around her waist, his closeness warm and secure. A different sort of shiver raced along her limbs.

She could only guess that he'd figured out that visiting the site of Lindsay's murder would be distressing. She wanted to lean into his comfort, to revel in the safety of his arms. But she had to steel herself. Relying on him wasn't a good idea. Not when their future was so precarious.

It took all of her willpower to step away from him and move with the group following Pat as he explained about the flags lining the walkway.

Zach stayed in step with her and leaned in close. "What do you think? Could he be the man you saw strangle Lindsay? I can't say either way if he's the same guy who broke into our house."

She grimaced. "I can't be sure, either. He seems more athletic than the attacker. His chin is a bit broader." Frustration throbbed at her temples. "I don't know."

He held her gaze for a beat then straightened and nodded as they moved along the walkway.

Eden could see why Pat was a popular tour guide. He was engaging, getting the crowd to laugh as he told stories of the park's history that she wasn't quite sure were true. He definitely was an entertainer.

Inside the Sculptor's Studio, where the artist Guzton Borglum worked from 1939 to 1941, the group gathered around the 1/12th scale model of Mount Rushmore while Pat presented a fifteen-minute talk focusing on the workers who'd helped Borglum create the monument and the tools and techniques they used. Eden could have recited the lecture by heart. Though Pat did have a dramatic flair and embellished a few points. Eden could only shake her head at the man's antics.

After Pat's lecture in the Sculptor's Studio, he led the group to the Grand View Terrace, saying they would resume their tour in thirty minutes, giving the group time to visit the Lincoln Borglum Visitor Center, where they could buy bottles of water, snacks or souvenirs.

Eden watched as Pat gravitated to a group of women ranging from early twenties to at least seventy. He was quite the charmer.

"I'm going take a run at him," Zach said.

Startled, she stared at Zach. "What do you mean?"

"Trust me." Zach winked and walked away.

Eden's heart sank. That was the problem. She did trust him. With her life. And that of their baby. But she couldn't stay married to a man who didn't want a family. A man who would only remain in their marriage out of duty and obligation, which would only lead to misery for them all.

Zach sauntered up next to Pat and studied the man through the sunglasses. There was no indication that Pat recognized him. But he could be as good actor. "You're hoarding all the ladies."

A twitter of giggles erupted from the women. A flash of irritation in Pat's gray eyes was the only suggestion that Zach was intruding. The man's smile broadened. "I think there's plenty to go around."

"I heard there's a secret room in the back of the monument," Zach said. "Will we get to see that?"

Pat's mouth thinned. "Ladies, if you'll excuse us."

Pat gestured for Zach to follow him, and they moved a few feet away beneath the shade of a bur oak.

"Unfortunately, tourists are not allowed in the secret room," Pat said. His eyes narrowed. "Do I know you?"

Zach put on his best smile. Had Pat seen him at the sheriff's station? "No, sir. This is my first time on a tour of the park." Which was technically true. Though he'd been here with Eden, had seen the evening program and traipsed through the woods outside the park boundaries, Zach had never been on a formal tour.

"Shouldn't you be attending to your lady friend?" Pat said, his gaze going to where Eden was sitting on a bench with her back to them. "She seems familiar, too."

Needing to redirect Pat's focus, Zach said conspiratorially, "You know how it is. Always need a backup plan."

A slow smile creased Pat's face. "True that. Nice to have a few on the line."

The man gave Zach the creeps. "Are you on the hunt for a new woman?"

Pat tucked in his chin and glared at Zach. "What makes you say that?"

"You sure were putting on the charm with those ladies. And I noticed the way you and the young lady ranger in the Sculptor's Studio were eyeing each other just before."

Anger glinted in Pat's gaze. "You don't know what you're talking about. Now, I should get back to the group." He stalked away.

Zach glanced at his watch. Their thirty minutes were almost up. Many of the tourists were talking freely among themselves and taking pictures. Keeping his eye on Pat, who, instead of heading to the group, ducked inside the visitor center, Zach moved back to Eden's side.

He wondered aloud, "Is there another way in and out of the park for employees?"

"Yes," Eden told him. "There are maintenance entrances that bypass the main gate."

Could Pat have ended his tour off-site, then come to the park in time to murder Lindsay and leave without being seen? Zach made a mental note to touch base with Sam to see if Pat's alibi checked out. He needed to catch Eden's attacker before further harm came to her and the baby—and time was running out.

TWELVE

Another ten minutes later, Pat corralled the group, intending to take them on the Presidential Trail, past the spot where Lindsay was murdered. Zach decided the man had a cold heart to so casually lead a tour past the area where the woman he had been dating had been killed.

Zach could see the panic flaring in Eden's eyes as they stared at the staircase. He tugged her to the side, letting others go ahead of them. "We don't have to do this."

"But I do," she said softly. "The sooner I face this, the better. I don't want to give up my job here. I love the park."

He knew she did and was glad he could be here with her facing the trauma of watching the young woman have her life strangled out of her. They moved up the steps toward the terrace, and the closer they got, the more Zach could feel the anxiety rushing off of Eden.

He reached down and threaded his fingers through hers. She twitched, her fingers flexing as she glanced at him. Then she nodded with a smile that sent his heart rate soaring.

He didn't want to give up this woman. Or the child she carried. But the fear of failing them was so strong, so consuming, that he just couldn't see a future for the three of them together. He wouldn't survive a repeat of the past. Especially if it was Eden or their baby that was hurt because of him.

Eden's heart rate ticked up as she and Zach and the other participants of the tour group neared the top of the Presidential Trail staircase, leading to the terrace where Lindsay Nash had been murdered. She clung to Zach's hand, probably crushing his fingers, but she couldn't let go even if she wanted to. He grounded her and kept her from losing control of her emotions.

Despite his reassuring presence, her steps faltered at the top as she stepped onto the terrace. She wished they'd been able to bring Amber with them—the dog was always a comfort—but non-service dogs weren't allowed in the park so Amber had to stay behind. The point of this exercise was to gather intel on Pat Dunbar.

A loose piece of bright yellow crime scene tape tied to the railing fluttered in the slight breeze. Pat must've seen the tape, as well, because he rushed to the railing to quickly untie the tape and stuff the yellow material into the pocket of his uniform.

Eden's gaze snagged on a particular section railing. The images of Lindsay being strangled tormented Eden. Her fingers went slack, releasing Zach's hand, and her breathing turned shallow.

Zach gripped her by the shoulders and turned her to face him. "Look at me," he said. "You're safe."

Holding his gaze to keep from looking at the spot where Lindsay had crumpled to the ground, she said, "It's just so awful."

"But you're facing it," Zach said. "I'm proud of you."

Buoyed by his words, she nodded and squared her shoulders. She was not going to let what happened yesterday destroy the career she'd built here at the park. If she did, then the killer would doubly win.

"Please, tell me you're going to find the villain who murdered Lindsay," she said.

Zach's solemn gaze filled with determination. "I'm going to do everything in my power to bring the killer to justice. And I'm going to keep you safe."

She believed him. One thing she'd learned in her year of marriage with him, he had a high sense of duty and unquenchable determination, which made him really good at search and rescue. Traits she appreciated and respected.

She began to relax.

They rejoined the group as Pat explained that,

because of the southeastern sun exposure that reflected off the mountain of rock, the sculptor had chosen the large granite edifice of Mount Rushmore for his project. Pat continued his tour, offering facts and stories about the area, until he finished with a flourish nearly thirty minutes later.

Eden's tummy rumbled as the group chatted and began to head out.

Beside her, Zach chuckled. "Somebody's hungry."

Unable to keep from smiling, she glanced up at him. "Perceptive of you."

Zach nodded and steered her away from the terrace. "Let's stop by the Carver Café on the way back to the office."

They made their way down the staircase on the other side of the Presidential Trail and headed to the park's eatery, where Eden bought a banana and a ginger ale.

After a quick stop at the ranger's station to collect Eden's things and say good-night to Matt, they made their way to the employee parking lot. Zach had parked his Pennington County Sheriff's vehicle next to Eden's compact sedan.

She climbed into the driver's seat of her car, but before she could shut the door, Zach gripped the edge and said, "I'll be right behind you. You remember how to get to the rental?"

She held up her phone. "I'll plug it into the GPS."

He gave her the address, which she typed into the phone, and soon she had the map function up with the blue line to follow. "All set."

He backed away. "Lock your doors."

Stifling the urge to roll her eyes at his overprotectiveness, she shut the door and made a show of deploying the lock. She waited until he was in his vehicle before she backed out of the parking spot and headed toward the highway.

In the rearview mirror, she saw Zach's vehicle pull out onto the highway and drop in behind her. She wished they were headed home to their own space, but the house had been too damaged in the fire. And sadly, they weren't together as a couple anymore, so going to the rental, a place that wasn't either of theirs, seemed appropriate.

Her phone rang and connected to the car's Bluetooth system. The phone screen showed her father's face. Affection swelled in her chest. Eden hit the button on the steering wheel that allowed her to answer the phone. "Hello, Daddy."

Karl Schaffer's deep voice filled the interior of the car. "Hi, honey, I just arrived at the airport in Nome, Alaska. My flight leaves in two hours. I'll be home by tomorrow afternoon. Are you okay?"

"I'm good," she said even as tears blurred her vision. She blinked them away and tightened her grip on the steering wheel. "Be safe, Daddy."

"I should be saying that to you, dear," he said. "It sounds like you're driving."

"Yes. I'm staying with Zach at his rental."

There was a moment of silence, then her father said, "Good. Zach will protect you until I can get there."

She did not doubt that Zach would keep her and the baby physically safe. But how was she going to protect her heart from her husband?

"You can go to the house if you'd rather," her father said.

The thought of retreating to her childhood home held appeal, but she didn't want to change the plan now. "I'll wait until you're back. I'm sorry you're cutting your trip short."

"Bah. The fish will be there next year," he said. "See you soon, honey."

She said goodbye to her father and glanced in the rearview mirror. A white work truck pulled into the oncoming traffic's lane to pass Zach's vehicle. Thinking to slow down and allow the truck to pass her, as well, she pumped the brakes, but nothing happened. She tried again, more urgently. Still nothing.

Panic shot through her. Someone had cut her brakes.

The sound of an engine revving grabbed Zach's attention as a white work truck with a ladder attached to the top sped up to pass him. He frowned as the vehicle drew abreast of him. Zach couldn't make out the driver's face through the truck's tinted windows. Then the truck shot forward, squeezing in between Zach and Eden.

Zach took his foot off the gas to allow his vehicle to slow.

The SUV's coolant light turned on seconds before a hissing sound came from the engine.

Zach hit the speed dial to connect with Eden to tell her his vehicle was overheating.

Her fear-filled voice sounded through the Bluetooth speakers. "Zach, my brakes aren't working!"

His heart stalled in his throat. "Use the emergency brake."

The work truck chose that moment to speed up and pull into the oncoming lane, looking as if it was going to pass Eden. But then the truck swerved, ramming into the side of her sedan and sending the car careening into the guardrail. Sparks flew from the metal hitting metal. Eden's scream, heard through his car speakers, froze the blood in his veins.

Gripping the steering wheel and barely breathing, Zach stepped on the gas, intending to wedge his SUV between the truck and Eden's sedan, but his overheating engine failed and the SUV slowed.

The work truck hit Eden's car again.

"Eden!"

The sedan broke through the guardrail and disappeared over the side of the road.

"No!" Zach stomped on the brakes and brought the SUV to a squealing halt. "Eden?" he shouted, but the call had disconnected.

The work truck raced away and disappeared out of sight around the next curve in the road.

Hitting the speed dial for Sam, Zach scrambled out of the SUV. He had to get to his wife and child.

Please, God, don't let them die.

The sedan traveled down the side of the gully, headed directly toward a large ponderosa. Eden's heart jammed in her throat. She spun the wheel, directing the car away from the tree, and yanked on the emergency brake, which locked up the tires, but the sedan continued to slide down the hill.

Though the car barely missed the tree, a grouping of granite boulders now loomed directly in front of her.

She braced for impact, covering her face with one hand and covering her baby with the other. The front end of the sedan rammed into the rocks.

The cacophony of noise from the violent crash of the car's front end meeting the immovable rocks shuddered through her. The airbag deployed with enough force to shove her into the backrest. Her hand stung from the blow. White powder puffed in the air, but the inflatable airbag kept her face from hitting the steering wheel.

When the world settled, the smell of gasoline assaulted her nose. Self-preservation compelled her to fling the driver's door open and climb out. Her legs wobbled, and she fell to her knees, forcing herself to crawl away from the wreckage seconds before the car exploded. A wave of heat scored over her back as she curled into a ball, protecting her head and her child.

"Eden!"

She uncurled enough to see Zach hurtling down the side of the embankment, panic and fear evident on his face. He dropped to his knees next to the inferno that had been her car, covering his face with his hands. His sobs rent the air.

He thought she'd died in the crash. Needing to let him know she was okay, she yelled, "Zach, here!"

His hands fell away from his face, and his tortured expression and confusion ripped through her heart. His gaze searched until he found her. His mouth opened and his eyes widened. She held his concern and relief-filled gaze.

He scrambled to his feet and ran for her. Dropping to the ground beside her, he gathered her close. His body shook like a leaf in the wind. "Are you hurt?"

"No, I don't think so." Her hand convulsed over

her tummy. She sent up a prayer of protection for the child she carried.

Zach placed kisses on her forehead, her nose and her cheeks, and finally, he captured her lips.

She sighed into the familiar sensation of her husband's kiss, but the scent of acrid smoke pulled her away.

"We have to call the fire department and the police," she said as she stared at the flames curling along the sides of her ruined sedan. As she watched, the grass beneath the wreckage caught fire. "The forest could burn. That truck deliberately ran me off the road. Someone cut my brake line. The driver of the van?"

"Logical conclusion." Zach took out his phone and made the necessary calls. When he was done, he put his phone away and gathered her close to his heart. "I'm glad you're okay. That you're both okay."

She clung to him, even knowing that his words were born of terror and a sense of duty. She couldn't trust his words or the sentiment behind them no matter how much she wanted his love. She wanted him to want their child. Without that… She put her hand over the baby she carried and prayed that somehow they would all survive the coming days.

Much to Zach's relief, Eden and the baby were declared unharmed at the hospital. Seeing the damage to Eden's car after it hit the boulder and witnessing the flames licking through the interior, he'd suffered a torment he never wanted to feel again. He'd come close to losing Eden. And their baby.

If they'd died...if anything happened to them, he'd never forgive himself.

They were his to protect. To care for. To lov— he couldn't bring himself to allow the word to fully form.

The fear of being responsible for another human being kept him from embracing the future Eden and their child offered. Shutting down his emotions, walling off his heart, was the best way, the only way, to really protect them.

He and Eden hitched a ride with Sam back to the rental house.

Zach's Sheriff's Department vehicle had been towed to the mechanic's workshop. They had determined that somebody had cut the radiator hose.

And from what Eden had experienced right before the crash, someone had cut the brake line on her sedan.

The work truck had been reported stolen from the park's maintenance shed, but it had been out of view of the security cameras. The perpetrator had obviously known the camera's blind spot. Someone like Pat Dunbar.

The truck was found miles away and there had been additional tire tracks near where the truck was found indicating another vehicle had been there. This attack on Eden was well planned out.

Zach couldn't keep the frustration from tightening the muscles in his neck or the acid from forming in his gut. Someone had gone to a lot of trouble to hurt Eden and keep him from being able to protect her. This level of determination to silence Eden seemed personal. If the guy was afraid of being caught for killing Lindsay, why not bug out and disappear?

As soon as they said goodbye to Sam, Eden had retreated to the bedroom, shutting the door, and shutting him out. It was just as well. He needed time to sort through what to do. And how to traverse the precarious nature of their circumstances.

Releasing Amber from the kennel, Zach walked outside, where he called Lucy for an update on the task force.

"West and I have been out with the dogs searching for the cachet of weapons that is supposedly somewhere here in the Black Hills," Lucy told him. "What's happening on your end? Is Eden doing okay?"

He relayed to her the events of the day.

"Whoa. Someone wants to harm Eden badly." Concern laced her words and echoed his earlier thoughts. "Do you need me to come be there with you guys?"

"We're good for now," Zach told Lucy. "We're going to lay low for a couple of days."

"Understood. Hey, Daniel called for a team meeting tomorrow. He wants a face to face with as many of us as can attend."

Blowing out a breath, Zach rubbed his free hand over his jaw. "I could probably make it." The Dakota Task Force headquarters was in Plains City, which was less than a half hour away from Keystone. "I'd have to bring Eden with me."

"I'm sure Daniel wouldn't mind," Lucy told him. "Let me know if there's anything I can do." She hung up.

Pocketing his phone, Zach whistled for Amber, who trotted over and waited for him to open the sliding glass door.

Inside the house, he found Eden sitting on the couch with the television on. Amber headed over to give her a greeting.

Eden hugged the dog and met Zach's gaze. "I wanted to see if the crash was on the news yet."

He sat down on the other end of the couch. There was a time when he would've sat next to her and taken her into his arms. But that time had passed. They were learning to operate within a new normal. And he hated it.

The news anchor's face filled the screen. "There's been another abduction in the Badlands." His tone was grim. A picture of a blonde woman appeared on the screen. "Our hopes and thoughts are with the family of the missing woman."

"Do you think the person who abducted these

women could be the same person who killed Lindsay? Was he trying to abduct Lindsay when I interrupted him?"

Though the task force was familiar with the abduction cases, Zach wasn't personally involved. From what he recalled, the first two women to be abducted were released a few days later but were unable to identify their assailant.

"I don't believe what happened in the park is related," he told her. "The abductions in the Badlands were of blonde women of a similar look. Lindsay was neither blonde nor a physical match to the other women who were taken." Since Lindsay didn't fit the type, it was unlikely that Eden had stumbled upon a serial kidnapper who was now trying to silence her.

Eden sighed. "I guess I should be relieved but I'm not. I'll add the missing woman to my prayers."

"As will I," he said.

Their shared faith had been one of the many bonds that had brought them together. Now he felt like he was letting God down. He rubbed his chin, feeling the bristle of the day against his palm. There hadn't been time to reach out to their pastor. As soon as Eden was no longer in jeopardy, he would seek Godly counsel. "Tomorrow I'll need to head to Plains City for a meeting."

She stared at him expectantly. "Okay."

"I'll need you to come with me," he said. "I'm not leaving you alone."

"Fine." She turned her face back to the television. Taylor crawled up onto Eden's shoulder and balanced on her collarbone, and her head rubbed against Eden's neck.

Zach almost likened the way Eden looked at him to a cat who had eaten the canary, except that she was holding Taylor and the tabby was looking at him with her big green eyes and no smile whatsoever. Sometimes Zach wasn't sure the feline approved of him.

When nothing about the crash appeared on the news report, Eden turned off the television. "I thought I would make some spaghetti for dinner. I noticed you have noodles and a jar of sauce in the cupboard. And a pound of hamburger in the refrigerator."

"Eden, you are not cooking." He jumped up from the couch. "I can make dinner. You're the one who needs to rest. You're the one that suffered the trauma."

He thought she'd protest, braced for it.

She held his gaze for a long moment. A gathering strength infused the depths of her green eyes, then she slowly nodded. "If you need any help, you let me know."

Gratified that she wasn't pushing herself, he went into the kitchen. As he went about the task of browning the meat and heating the noodles and sauce, he thought about the dinners they'd shared over the past year. He missed the easy camaraderie he'd had with his wife.

He tried to imagine a year from now. They'd be living separate lives. Her with their child. Would they have a boy or a girl?

His heart ached.

Living separate lives wasn't what he wanted.

Gripping the edge of the counter, fear washed over him. Could he tame the terror of parenthood to live a full life with his wife and child?

THIRTEEN

The next morning Eden dressed in a nice pair of slacks and a complementing blouse. She was a bit nervous to meet the Dakota Gun Task Force boss and the other team members. These people were important to Zach and were big-time law enforcement personnel doing a job that served all of the Dakotas. She wanted to make a good impression. She wasn't sure what Zach had told them about her or their marriage.

She understood why Zach wanted her to come with him to Plains City. And frankly, she wasn't up for staying alone. Or going back to the office at Mount Rushmore. She would be safe within the Plains City police building, where both the task force and the ATF had their headquarters.

When she left her room, Zach and Amber were already at the SUV.

Joining them, she admired him in his tan uniform. He was so handsome, tall and fit. Her heart ached. To cover her reaction, she smoothed a hand over her hair. She'd brushed it out and used a small clip to hold back one side. She caught Zach watching her, his expression unreadable.

"Is this okay?" She hated needing the reassurance but couldn't stop from asking.

"You're beautiful." He reached past her to open the passenger door.

His compliment made her smile, as did his courteous manners.

On the way out of Keystone, they stopped at the diner and grabbed coffee to go along with savory breakfast sandwiches.

From the back compartment, Amber whined as Eden munched on her ham and cheese croissant.

"Is it okay if I give her a piece?" she asked Zach. She'd seen him give the dog human food on occasion. But she still wasn't versed on what the dog could or could not have.

"Sure," Zach said. "Just be prepared. Once you start feeding her by hand she's going to want it more often."

Eden smiled. If giving the dog a bite meant that Amber and Zach were going to be around, she would gladly hand-feed the dog every meal. But she hesitated before handing the dog a corner of the sandwich as her emotions warred within her chest. She was so conflicted. On one hand, she wanted Zach and Amber to stay in her life. Wanted them to be a family in every way. Yet, on the other hand, she knew Zach was going to leave her as soon as the threat to her life was over.

She didn't want him to stay out of obligation.

Either way, she hoped that Amber would enjoy the special treat. Eden offered it through the grate in the dog's compartment. The black Lab gobbled it up.

There was little traffic between Keystone and Plains City and they reached the brick four-story building on the corner block in Plains City, South Dakota without delay. Zach drove around to the back and parked. He pointed to a building off to the side. "That is our training facility."

Eden looked across the expanse of lawn with picnic tables to the building Zach indicated. "Do you have your own veterinarian there, as well?"

"We do. She is top-notch. So are the trainers. We'll let Amber hang out there while we're in the meeting."

He led the way to the building and opened the back door with a key fob, and they entered.

The large open space had a small arena with equipment such as jumps, tunnels, a fake window and what Eden would compare to a balance beam like she'd walked in her gymnastic classes in high school. Off to one side was a long row of kennels outside of several offices. Eden noted that one office had the name of the veterinarian stenciled on the door.

Amber seemed happy to greet the trainers, several of whom were working with dogs of various breeds.

One woman of about forty, with short, bobbed hair and glasses, broke away and took Amber's lead from Zach. "We'll take good care of her. We have a few of the other dogs, too."

"Thanks," Zach said. "It shouldn't be too long."

Eden and Zach left the dog in the trusted hands of the K-9 training center.

As they crossed the expanse of grass, Zach paused to look at his watch. "We're a bit early." He gestured to the picnic table. "Did I tell you about the abandoned toddler that was found right here?"

Eden's eyebrows went up. Surprised crimped her chest. "No, you did not."

"Two months ago, West and another officer, Trish McCord, found a toddler abandoned here on this picnic bench. She had a note pinned to her chest that said 'My name is Joy. I'm agent Daniel Slater's kin.'"

"Wow, that's amazing," Eden said. "What was the relation?"

"We didn't know at first. But after a rapid DNA test, Daniel discovered she was a relation on his father's side. As far as Daniel knew, he only had his grandmother. And she didn't know who the child was, either."

Empathy for the child filled her. "What happened to the little girl?"

"Daniel took her in, and his grandmother is

taking care of her while they search for her parents."

"I can't imagine how distressing it must be for your boss. Why would someone just leave a toddler behind like that?" She reflexively put her hand to her tummy, silently vowing she'd never abandon her child.

"That's something we are all wondering." He started walking again. At the back door of the main building, he used his key fob once again to open the door.

Inside, he led the way to a conference room.

Eden hesitated at the door. Peering inside, she saw Lucy and West, whom she knew. But the others she didn't. Her nerves made her hands shake. "I don't think I should go in there. Do they have an employee lounge where I could wait?"

A tall man with dark blond hair and bright green eyes pushed open the door all the way. "Zach," the man said. "I'm glad you could join us." His gaze zeroed in on Eden. "You must be Eden."

"I must," she said nervously and shook the hand he stuck out.

"I'm Daniel Slater," he said. "This one's boss for now." He released her hand and stepped aside. "Both of you, please take a seat."

"Are you sure?"

Daniel nodded. "We won't be discussing anything confidential."

Feeling like she was facing a strange new world, Eden took a breath and stepped inside.

Zach placed his hand against Eden's lower back and felt the tremor working its way through her. Knowing she felt uncomfortable being included in the briefing, he guided her toward the back of the room where there was seating out of the way. "Will this do?"

The grateful smile she gave him warmed his heart. She nodded and sank into the seat.

Zach stepped forward to sit in the seat in front of her at the large oval table. At least here, he knew that they didn't have to worry about anyone trying to harm her.

He glanced around the table, nodding to his fellow task force members. Lucy and West sat on the opposite side of the table from him. In the seat next to him was Liam Barringer, an FBI agent from Bismarck who specialized in homicide. He had a male bloodhound named Guthrie who specialized in cadaver detection. Though, like Amber, Guthrie was at the training center.

Then there was Jenna Morrow, a Fargo K-9 patrol officer who had a male German shepherd named Augie, who specialized in suspect apprehension and was cross-trained in most basic scent detection. Augie sat at Jenna's feet. Some dogs did not like to be kenneled or to be left behind. Apparently, Augie was one of them.

Also present was Aurora Martin, the task force's and the Plains City Police Department's crime scene investigator. Beside her was another Plains City K-9 officer, Jack Donadio. Jack had been injured recently so was on desk duty helping out with warrants and such. Zach recalled seeing Jack's K-9, a male black Lab specializing in electronic detection, at the training center earlier. Cheyenne Chen, the team's tech analyst, wasn't in the room, which likely meant she was hard at work on a lead and would join the meeting when she could.

Daniel was an ATF supervisory special agent with a Great Dane named Dakota. They both moved to the head of the table. Dakota settled on the floor beside where Daniel stood.

The task force was short one member—Gracie Fitzpatrick out of the Plains City US Marshals office. She had gone into witness protection with a man she had been recently protecting. Zach had no idea where they'd ended up and hoped they were well.

Having Gracie gone left them with an open seat at the table. Zach wondered who would join them.

"Okay, everyone settle down," Daniel said. "We have several things to go over."

A couple people shifted in their seats to face their boss.

"Update on the trafficking ring," Daniel said. "Lucy and Zach have interviewed the ex-girlfriend of Jared Olin. She provided a photo of Olin and a man referred to as Brandon. We don't have a last name for him yet. Cheyenne and Jack are in the process of searching all databases for a hit."

Zach had every confidence the team's tech analyst would come up with an ID.

"We do know that the photo was taken in front of the Plains City Pizzeria where West witnessed Jared Olin and Petey Pawners with illegal weapons. The photo has turned out to be a great lead. Hopefully, once we identify the man in the photo, we'll be that much closer to bringing these gun traffickers to justice."

Congratulations for acquiring the photo were given to Lucy and Zach from those in the room. Zach felt heat rise up his neck. He glanced over his shoulder at Eden. She smiled at him with pride. Her approval did funny things to his insides. He wanted to reach out and take her hand, but instead faced the front again.

"Daniel, any information you can share on the toddler, Joy?" Jenna asked. The whole team had been curious about the child since she'd been left at DGTF headquarters.

"Yes. Though we have a lead on the child's mother, a woman named Serena Rogers," Daniel said. "We are having trouble locating her. I'm sure something will surface soon."

There were murmurs of empathy that ran through the room. Like Eden had expressed earlier, Zach couldn't understand why somebody would abandon their child.

The thought nearly wrecked him. Because wasn't that what he was essentially doing by continuing to hold on to his fear? Something to think about later. Now he concentrated as Daniel cleared his throat.

"On another matter that's more personal to all of us here," Daniel said, his voice filling with emotion. "Our fallen colleague Kenyon Graves's birthday is coming up. He would've been thirty-three years old. His life was cut too short. I know each and every one of you have vowed to make sure that those who perpetrated the crime are brought to justice."

Vocal agreements swept through the room. Kenyon had died too young at the hands of the gun traffickers they were chasing. The task force wouldn't let the criminals get away with it. Those responsible would serve time for both the smuggling and the murder charges. Still, Zach's heart ached for the three-year-old twin boys Kenyon had left behind, who were now being raised by a family friend. This job came with risks—if anything ever happened to him, he'd be putting Eden and their unborn child in the same position. The thought squeezed his heart and left him needing to catch his breath.

"In light of his impending birthday, we would like to honor Kenyon with a celebration of life gathering. Though we've put his picture up on our wall of fallen heroes, we haven't done an official memorial."

Taking a calming breath, Zach voiced his agreement. "That's a fabulous idea." Though he hadn't known Kenyon Graves personally, he knew that his fate could befall any of them at any time. It would mean something to his family, his sons, to honor him.

"I'll help plan the celebration," West volunteered.

Zach knew that West and Kenyon had been best friends.

The door to the conference room opened, and Cheyenne stepped inside. She was tall and slim with dark hair and dark eyes. "Sorry, I'm late."

"Anything to report?" Daniel asked.

"Not yet, but I'm close," she said. Her gaze turned to the crime scene investigator in the room with a nod.

Aurora sat up straighter. "I've managed to lift viable DNA evidence off of the weapons found by West and Trish. Cheyenne has been running it through CODIS."

"Good job," Daniel said. "When you have more, please let us know. Until then you are all dismissed."

Zach scooted his chair back and turned so that he faced Eden. He held out his hands. He was gratified when she placed her hands in his.

"We'll let everybody else get out of here before we leave," he told her.

"I appreciate that," she said. "But honestly, I'd like to meet your colleagues. You're right. They all seem like wonderful people."

He was glad to hear her say that. He stood, and she rose beside him. Before too many people left the room, he introduced her to Aurora, Liam and Cheyenne.

Each expressed their pleasure to meet her and their upset that she was in danger.

Cheyenne gave Eden a hug. "I can only imagine what you're going through. But you have the best team in your corner."

"Yes, I do," Eden said, her gaze meeting Zach's. He could feel his chest puff up at having her praise.

If only she could look at him with such warmth always. But if he ever told her the truth about his past, she would turn away from him in disgust.

They hurried out of the building and across the grass to the training center, where they found Amber running through an obstacle course with one of the trainers.

"That looks like fun," Eden said.

"It is, both for the dog and the human."

When Amber jumped over the last hurdle, she raced to Zach's side and sat with a happy grin, her tongue rolling out the side of her mouth. He reached into his utility belt and gave her several treats.

He waved his thanks to the trainer and then escorted Amber and Eden to his vehicle. The ride back to Keystone was pleasant and thankfully uneventful. They stopped at the diner to get takeout.

For a moment, Zach could almost pretend that they were just a normal couple, happy and in love. Unfortunately, there was too much at risk for either of them to let down their guard.

Another child had gone missing. Eden's heart dropped and the food she'd just eaten curled in her gut. The call came in after lunch a couple days later.

This one was a case of a two-year-old wandering off while on a trip to Custer State Park with her father.

Eden had insisted that Zach take her to her father's house. As much as she appreciated Zach's diligence in protecting her and their unborn baby, the missing child needed him and Amber more at the moment. She imagined the little one was scared, and her soon-to-be mother's heart wanted to bring the child home to her parents right away. She wished there was some way she could help as she watched Zach gear up.

Agitation revved through her veins. Two missing children in a short amount of time. Search and rescue operations seemed to escalate during the summer months because more people were venturing out into the beautiful forest and parks of South Dakota.

Eden knew it could only take a moment for a fast-moving child to disappear from a distracted parent. She'd witnessed it happen at Mount Rushmore many times over the years.

Zach drove them to a residential area on the other side of town, where she'd grown up with her dad and mom, until her passing. The tree-lined street filled on either side by older homes with expansive yards brought a smile to Eden. She remembered riding her bike up and down the street with the neighbor kids in the summers and snowball fights in the winter. It had been an idyllic place to grow up.

All the families had been friendly, and when her mom had been ill, the neighborhood rallied around Eden and her dad. They'd never lacked for casseroles or someone to shovel the snow or mow the grass. And after her mother's death, the women in the neighborhood had often stopped in to check on her and her father.

Her childhood home sat closer to the curb than most of the homes, because when her parents had had the house built, they'd wanted more backyard than front. According to them, a family's life happened in the backyard because that's where the children could play freely. But she'd still ended up out front in the street with all the other kids.

Though, her parents had hosted many barbecues in the backyard, until her mom's sickness robbed her of her strength.

When she and Zach arrived at the house, they found her father waiting on the raised wooden porch. As a former sheriff, Eden knew her father would protect her with his life. Karl Schaffer was a big man in his late fifties with dark graying hair and a warm smile. Eden loved her father. He'd been the rope that had kept them from coming untethered after her mother's death.

When Zach made to get out of the vehicle, she stopped him with a hand on his arm. "Don't waste time here with me. Go. Find the missing child. That's what you do, Zach. You protect children. I will be praying for the child. And you."

A shadow passed behind his eyes. He covered her hand with his own. The callous from Amber's lead scraped across her skin. He lifted her knuckles to his lips and kissed them. "Thank you, Eden. Please don't go anywhere."

Swallowing back emotions clogging her throat, she nodded before hopping out of the vehicle and stepping away. Zach backed the SUV out of the driveway and sped off toward Custer State Park to find the missing child. She had no doubt they'd be successful. They had to be.

Please, Lord, no tragedies today.

FOURTEEN

Eden hurried to her father and fell into his bear hug. He smelled of the spices from his aftershave. The scent brought back memories from her childhood.

Keeping one arm around her, he led her inside the house. "You're here now. You're safe."

"It's all just such a mess, Daddy," she said and burst into tears.

"Hey, now, what has Zach done this time?"

That wasn't fair. She couldn't let her dad think Zach was fully responsible for the predicament they were in. Hiccupping with tears, she said, "Nothing. He's been great. Protective and attentive." She took a shuddering breath. "Things are complicated."

"Let's go inside and you can tell me all about it," Karl said.

Eden fought to gain control of her emotions as she went inside the house. She noted with surprise a new leather couch stood where the old gold and brown upholstered sofa had once been, and a large-screen television mounted on the living room wall had replaced the dark oak television cabinet. It was so unlike her father to make a change.

For years he'd kept the house exactly as it had been when her mother was alive. Eden had had to badger her father into replacing the dining room table when one of the legs had broken a few years ago.

Wiping away her tears, she said, "I like the couch. What brought on this change?"

Karl gestured for her to sit. "It was time."

Taking a seat on the buttery soft leather couch, Eden ran her hand over the closer of two velvety soft patterned throw pillows. "Since when do you have decorative pillows?"

Was her father blushing? "Those were a gift."

Eden's breath stalled. "A gift." Only a woman would pick out such an item. "Who?"

Clearing his throat, Karl took a seat beside Eden. "I'm seeing Leslie Perkins."

"The elementary school librarian?" Eden had known Mrs. Perkins her whole life. She had been a widow longer than her father had been a widower.

"Yes. I meant to tell you before I left on the fishing trip, but you were so upset about Zach…" He trailed off.

Stunned, Eden searched her heart and decided

she was happy for her father. He deserved to find love again. "I think it's great, Daddy."

"I'm glad," Karl said, his relief evident. He took her hand. "Has there been another attempt on your life?"

"No, not in a few days." Remembering the panic at losing control of her car sent a shudder of fear coursing over her flesh. "I—I'm pregnant."

For a moment, he didn't speak. Then a wide grin spread across his face, and he let out a loud whoop. He wrapped his arms around her and hugged her close. "I'm so excited."

Happiness bubbled up. "Me, too."

He pulled back to stare into her face. "But Zach isn't."

She shook her head. "I don't understand why he's so against having children."

"Hmm," Karl said. "Have you asked him?"

"Yes, of course." She couldn't keep the sharpness from her tone. "He says it's a big responsibility that he's not sure he could handle. And that too many things could go wrong. It doesn't make sense. He's the most responsible person in my life, besides you, and he should know there are no guarantees in life. He'll be a great dad. He's so kind and loving. Gentle with children. I've seen him with those he's rescued. The way the little ones trust him."

"Have you told him all of this?"

Her shoulders drooped. "No." Instead, she'd let

hurt and pride take over. She'd lashed out instead of pointing out his strengths.

"You need to tell him how you feel and press him to get to the heart of his fear," Karl said.

Eden stared at her father, sensing the comment wasn't random. "Is there something you know that I don't?"

"It's not my story to tell, honey." Karl stood. "Let's have a snack. I'm famished."

Putting her hand over her abdomen, Eden wondered what exactly was Zach's story? And why hadn't he shared whatever it was with her?

Fresh tears stung her eyes. Did he not trust her? Was that the real reason he wanted out of their marriage? Her heart folded in on itself at the thought.

Zach arrived at Custer State Park and pulled his SUV behind Sam's vehicle. A group of law enforcement and park rangers congregated near the trailhead.

Zach let Amber out and hooked her up to the long leash. The dog sniffed the air. Her whole body vibrated with energy. She knew they were going to work. They hustled over to the group.

"We have a problem," Sam informed him.

"A missing child isn't problem enough?" Zach frowned. The grim expression on his friend and colleague's face didn't bode well. Zach really couldn't take a loss right now. "Where are the parents? We need a piece of clothing or something of the child's."

"That's the problem," Sam said. "The child's parent has disappeared."

Frustration tore through Zach. "He's gone off looking for his kid on his own?" The adult might get lost also, and then they'd have two people to search for and rescue.

"Not sure," Sam replied, turning to the nearest park ranger. "This is Ranger David Bowles. He was the first to be informed of the lost child."

Ranger Bowles had a thin mustache and dark eyes that didn't quite focus on Zach. "Yeah, I got the call that there was a missing child. I came right over. I talked to the father and told him I would bring reinforcements. He demanded I call the sheriff's search and rescue team. So I did."

A buzzing started at the back of Zach's mind. "Where did he lose track of his child?"

Bowles pointed toward the trailhead. "He said a couple of miles up the trail."

Zach glanced around. "Where did he go?"

Bowles shrugged. "Don't know. I told him to wait here at the trailhead while I radioed the Sheriff's Department from my vehicle. When I came back, he was gone. I can only imagine he started up the trail."

Shaking his head, Zach asked, "Do you know which vehicle he arrived in?" Amber could get a scent off of the door handle if the vehicle was locked.

"That's the thing," Bowles said. "When I arrived, there weren't any vehicles in the parking lot. I don't know how he and his child got here."

The buzzing in Zach's mind became a roar. "Something about this doesn't feel right," Zach said. But a child could be in danger. They couldn't just dismiss the claims of a reckless, distraught parent. "Maybe they live close enough to walk to the park. Amber and I are going to head out." Zach turned to Sam. "I'll keep you informed via radio. There's not much cell service in the park."

"I'll come with you," Sam said.

"Ranger Bowles can come with us," Zach said. "Since he's already seen the guy and can identify him." He trusted Amber would pick up any fresh trails and hopefully lead them to either the child or the dad. She could also lead them to anyone else in the park. Tracking from a scent article was more precise than air scent tracking. Either way they had to get moving.

"Sure, I can go with you," Bowles said.

"Roger that," Sam said. "Check in often. I don't want to have to come searching for you guys, too."

Zach and Amber, with Ranger Bowles in tow, headed up the trailhead through Custer State Park. Zach lifted up a prayer that they would find the child and the parent quickly. And not just for their sake. He needed to get back to Eden.

In the sunny yellow guest bathroom that had once been exclusively Eden's, she splashed water on her face to wash away her tears. Telling her father about the baby had been cathartic. His excitement touched her deeply. Though learning that Zach held some part of himself back from her hurt and pricked her pride. Boy, she sure had an issue with those two emotions. Was she being too sensitive? Taking his lack of disclosure too personally? But weren't a husband and wife supposed to share all aspects of their lives? What was it about her that made him not want to open up?

Curiosity ate at her, but she would have to wait until he'd found the missing child and returned to her. It seemed at every turn God was forcing her to exercise patience. A skill she supposed she'd need as a new parent.

She dried her face and then wandered down the hall to her old bedroom. She'd long ago stripped most of her belongings from the walls and had replaced the flowered print bed set from her youth. The room now was nearly bare, with a few fragments left of her childhood. A well-loved teddy bear sat on the dark blue bedspread. She was surprised to see a set of framed photos of her mother sat on the white bedside table. Her father must have added them. She picked up one of the pictures as longing washed through her. She missed her mother.

Leaving the photo where she'd found it, she pulled her phone from her pocket and checked it. Nothing from Zach. Keeping the device gripped in one hand, she walked out on the back porch, where her father was seated drinking a glass of lemonade. She took a seat on the lounge chair next to him. He gestured to the glass on the knee-high table. "Yours."

"Thanks." She picked up the glass with her free hand and drank, letting the tart and sweet liquid fill her with more nostalgia. Sitting here with a view of the expansive backyard, filled with the roses her mother had planted and the birdhouses her father had built over the years, had always been her favorite place to be.

As much as she wanted to relax, she couldn't shake the tension as she clutched her phone, waiting for news of the child that Zach was searching for. He'd promised to let her know when they found the missing toddler. It was always so nerve-racking when a person went missing. Especially a child. Her hand went reflexively to her stomach.

Her phone dinged with an incoming text, and she quickly checked the screen. She didn't recognize the number. Wary but curious, she swiped to open it and read the text.

This is Julie. I need to speak to you. I'm taking Sweet Pea for a good long walk. Can you meet me at Willow Creek Trail?

Eden stared at the request. Why was Julie leaving the safety of the women's shelter? What did she need to talk to Eden about? Willow Creek Trail was one of many in a labyrinth of trails that wound through the Black Hills National Forest. She and Zach had hiked it often, and of late Eden and Julie had taken to the trail.

"What is it, honey?" Concern darkened her father's deep green eyes.

She explained the situation to him about Julie and her husband, Jon Fielding. "She wants me to meet her at the trailhead where we usually go for hikes."

"She sounds like she's in need of a friend." Dad peered at her, searching her face. "Are you up for a hike?"

"Maybe a short one, but I should wait until I hear from Zach."

"It could be a while," her dad said. "It might be good for you to meet with your friend. I'll take you. I won't let anything happen to you."

"I would like to make sure she's okay," Eden said. "But I'll let her know I'm not up for much of a hike. We can meet her in the parking lot. We can talk before she takes her dachshund for a walk."

"Then let's get a move on." Dad rose from the lounge chair and headed inside.

Eden sent off a text telling Julie she'd meet her but that she wouldn't be able to go for a walk.

An incoming text dinged.

That's fine. I just need a moment of your time. Please come alone. I don't want anyone, especially Jon, to know that you're meeting me.

Hesitating, she understood Julie's concern and why she didn't want her husband to know where she was. Eden typed back.

I promise there's no way Jon could find out we're meeting from me. I'll see you soon.

Three dots appeared and then disappeared. Feeling like she was doing something productive and that would keep her mind off Zach, Eden tucked her phone into her pocket and hurried to get into her dad's pickup truck.

As soon as Eden settled in the passenger seat and had the seat belt buckle fastened, her father backed out of the driveway and headed toward the highway that would take them to the hiking trail at Willow Creek.

"Did you text Zach?" her dad asked.

"No, but I should. I just don't want to distract him from finding that missing child," she said lifting up a silent prayer for the child in question. The family had to be frantic.

She breathed in deep, putting her hand over her tummy. A queasy sort of terror struck her heart.

"Zach's a professional," her father said, his voice stern. "As long as you make it clear that I am with you, he has nothing to worry about. But he deserves to know what's happening. He's your husband and the father of your child."

Her father was right, of course.

"As soon as we get to the trailhead, I'll text him," she said. "Looking at my phone while in a moving vehicle tends to make my motion sickness worse. Especially now that I'm expecting."

"I know you and Zach are having a difficult time because you wanted a family and he didn't," her father said softly. "But the decision has been taken out of both of your hands. God has brought this child into your lives. You two need to work it out."

"You make it sound so simple," she said. "Zach said he could adapt to having a family. What does he mean, *adapt*? He'll stay in our marriage, but only out of duty and honor. Not out of love or desire to be a father and a husband. I can't live like that, Dad. I won't live like that."

"Have you prayed about it?"

"Of course, I have," she said. "But I know God's not a genie who's going to grant me my wishes."

"True. God is not a genie. But the things that we humans think are impossible are not impossible for God. Give Zach time to come to terms with what he can't control. Give him some grace."

"I'm trying," she said. "I'm just not so good at it. I just don't understand his aversion of parenthood. I get that it's scary. Anything could happen at any moment. But if I thought the way he does, I never would've married a man who was in law enforcement." She turned her gaze on her father. "How did Mom feel about you being sheriff?"

"Your mom was a woman of prayer," he said. "She knew in this life there would be trials. She prayed for my safety every day. She prayed I would come home to her every night. And I prayed I would come home to her every night."

Eden swallowed back the sorrow rising up to choke her. "But she was the one who ended up dying. She was the one who left us."

A muscle worked in her father's strong jaw, clearly fighting the pain of their shared grief. "We never know what's coming or what will befall us," he said softly. "What we do know, what your mother and I knew, was that our lives and your life and Zach's life and your baby's life are safe in God's hands. Whether here on earth or in heaven."

She wanted to take solace in the words. But she just didn't know if she was strong enough. She didn't have her father's broad shoulders to bear the burden of loss. Thinking about something happening to her child, whether before she gave birth or after, filled her with a panicky tremor so wide and so deep she wasn't sure she could withstand the trials her father talked about. "Zach's terrified. And now I'm terrified."

"Then you be terrified together," her father said firmly. "And trust in God."

"Is that how you survived Mom's death?"

"Yes, with a lot of help from our pastor and friends and you," he said.

"Me? I was a basket case for years," she admitted.

"You were. Which helped ground me." Her father sighed. "Before your mother passed, she and I had a very frank heart-to-heart conversation. We knew the end was coming. She had run her race and it was a good race. But it was time for her to stop. I didn't want it. And I railed against God." A big fat tear rolled down her father's cheek as he kept his focus on the road.

Eden choked up, her own tears flowing freely now.

"But your mother, she was steadfast and faithful as any woman God ever created," he said. "She made me promise that I would live my life and run my race until the very end. And that I would make sure you did the same."

Eden wiped away the tears streaming down

her cheeks. "I've never understood that part of Scripture that said that we have a race to run."

"What the apostle Paul is talking about is that each of us, individually, have our own journey. You have yours, just as Zach has his. There are things in his past that he has had to overcome. But those things have shaped him. Just as your mother's death shaped you. You are strong and resilient. You are running your race with authenticity."

Shifting her gaze to the forest passing by outside the truck's window, Eden replayed her father's words, trying to digest and unpack each sentence. Her mother's death had shaped her. She had become more appreciative and grateful for the people in her life.

And more willing to take risks.

Like marrying a man she'd only met two months prior to her wedding day. A man she'd thought she'd known. But perhaps not. She thought about conversations she'd had with her husband, filtering through the words, wanting to know if she'd missed something. Maybe clues to a past she clearly didn't know.

Finally, she looked back at her father and asked, "What things are in Zach's past, Dad?"

"As I said before, that's a discussion you'll need to have with Zach." He turned on the blinker and pulled into the parking lot for the Willow Creek trailhead. There were two other cars in the parking lot. Neither of them she recognized. Maybe Julie had bought a new car?

Sitting in the cab of the truck, Eden searched the area for signs of her friend. Had Julie set off on the hike without her? Or could she be in the restrooms?

Eden popped open the door, and her father stopped her with a hand on her arm. "Zach. Text."

She'd almost forgotten. She quickly sent off a text to Zach telling him she was with her dad and they were at Willow Creek Trail so that she could meet with Julie Fielding. She said she would text him when they were on their way home.

"I'm going to check the restrooms," she said.

"I'll come with," her father said.

Without waiting for her to agree, her father climbed out of the driver's seat and slammed the door. Eden followed her father to the park's facilities. At the threshold to the women's restroom, she held up a hand. A moment of déjà vu struck her and she smiled. "No need to come in, Dad. I'll scream if there's trouble."

Her father shrugged and moved to the park bench a couple feet away. He leaned against the edge of the table like the former sheriff he was, his cowboy booted feet crossed and his arms over his chest.

Eden's heart swelled with her love for him as she ducked into the women's restroom. The one room stall was empty. There was a note written in lipstick on the mirror.

Headed up the trail. J.

Shock and irritation darkened Eden's spirit. She'd told Julie she wasn't going for a hike. Of course, she hadn't explained why she wasn't up for taking the trail, but what if she hadn't gone into the restroom?

Shaking her head, she walked out of the building.

Her father was nowhere to be seen.

FIFTEEN

"Dad!"

Panic revved in Eden's veins. Where was her father? She glanced at the truck, hoping maybe he'd decided to sit inside the cab to wait, but the truck was empty.

The jingle of a bell caught Eden's attention. She caught sight of Julie's little dachshund dragging its pink-colored leash as the dog ran up the trail.

After quickly looking into the men's restroom and finding no one, Eden debated her options. Did she go up the trail and hope the dog led her to Julie and her father? Or should she wait for Zach? That could be hours. He could be in the middle of Custer State Park without cell service.

She sent off a text to Lucy Lopez, Zach's colleague, asking for help. Then she headed up the trail in search of the dog, Julie and her father, the whole time praying she found them all alive.

Tension born of frustration cramped the muscles in Zach's shoulders as he followed Amber as she searched for a scent along the winding, rock-lined Badger Clark Historic Trail through Custer State Park.

They'd been at it for over an hour, passing many interpretive signs highlighting the landscape and the life of Charles Badger Clark, South Dakota's first poet laureate. The sun, high in the sky, beat down on them. Sweat dripped down his back beneath his tan uniform shirt and black Kevlar vest.

Amber sniffed at the tall grass and shrubs growing at the edges of the trail, beneath the forest's mix of pine and hardwood trees. Her body language was relaxed and unhurried with no indication of fresh human scent.

What did the lack of a discernable trace mean? Had they missed where the child and father had gone into the woods? Or would they pick up the scent farther up ahead? Or was there even a missing child and father?

A distinct low rumbling sound echoed through the trees. Recognizing the noise as that of a male bison announcing its presence, Zach paused. Amber lifted her head and stared in the direction from which the noise emanated.

Ranger Bowles wiped his brow with the back of his hand. "Last I knew the herd's on the other side of the park. The noise carries."

Zach waited to hear the more guttural warnings of threat that bison used to signal to the herd, but the rumbling stopped. The forest quieted. Though he couldn't see the large mammals through the tall pines, that didn't mean the creatures couldn't be nearby eating the shrubs or rubbing their furry bodies against the tree trunks to rid themselves of insects.

Clicking into his cheek to give Amber the signal to take a break, Zach pulled his phone from his pocket, intending to call Sam, and saw that he had a missed text from Eden.

He opened the text app and read.

Dad and I are going to Willow Creek Trail to meet Julie. Will text when done.

Zach frowned. He'd told her to stay put. While he trusted her father to protect her, an ominous tightness developed in his chest. What was Karl doing taking her away from the house? Why were they meeting with Julie?

"I'm calling it," Zach said to Ranger Bowles. "Let's head back."

The other man nodded his agreement, and they turned and began retracing their steps down the trail with Zach setting a brisk pace.

Ranger Bowles mused, "I don't understand it. The guy was frantic. But also a little strange. I'm mean, why would a dad intending to go on a hike with his kid wear a leather bomber jacket on such a warm day?"

"Bomber jacket?" Alarm bells went off in Zach's head. The man he'd confronted and had a fight with inside his and Eden's home had had on a bomber jacket. "What did you say the guy looked like?"

"Over six feet. He wore mirrored sunglasses." Ranger Bowles scoffed. "Blond. In need of a haircut."

Acid burned through Zach's stomach. The description matched Lindsay Nash's killer. The same man who'd attacked Eden. And most likely the same man who had tried to burn down their home and who ran Eden off the road.

His heart rate picked up, and Zach increased the pace until he was running back down the trail.

Beside him, Ranger Bowles kept up. "What's happening?"

"This was a setup. It had to be. You were asked to call specifically for search and rescue," Zach said between panic-tinged breaths. "He knew I'd come and leave Eden alone. I have to get to my wife."

Amber barked and raced ahead of Zach. The dog understood Zach's urgency. Amber had an uncanny way of tuning in to her handler's energy. When she reached the end of the lead of the tracking harness, she slowed and looked over her shoulder at Zach. He did his best to keep up with her.

By the time they reached the trailhead, Zach

was winded but the agitation zooming through his system amped his energy level. Sam and another deputy waited. As Amber, Zach and Ranger Bowles thundered toward them, Sam held up a hand. "Whoa. Do we need an ambulance?"

Zach slowed and bent to place his hands on his knees while trying to catch his breath. "No. It's Eden."

"Explain." There was no mistaking the concern in Sam's tone.

Zach straightened and pointed to Ranger Bowles. "The supposed panicked dad sounds too similar to the man targeting Eden."

Sam's gaze widened. "We can send a patrol out to pick her up. Where is she?"

"I got a text saying she was heading to Willow Creek Trail, near Mount Rushmore, with her father." Zach moved toward his vehicle. "She's supposedly meeting her friend Julie Fielding."

Matching his stride, Sam asked, "Neighbor Julie?"

"Yes, neighbor Julie, who supposedly left her abusive husband," Zach said. "Eden's text came in over an hour ago."

"We have no reason to believe they are in danger," Sam pointed out.

"Amber tracked the man who broke into our home to the Fieldings' residence," Zach said. "It still could be Pat Dunbar. Do we know his whereabouts? But what if Jon Fielding is the man who wants Eden dead?"

"We've already looked at Fielding. And I'll check on Dunbar," Sam commented as they drew to a stop at Zach's vehicle. "We can certainly look at both men again."

Given the timing of the fake missing child and the text from Julie, Zach was certain he knew the identity of the killer.

"My gut's telling me Jon's our guy." Zach put Amber in her compartment, shut the door and turned to stare at his friend. "I have a bad feeling, Sam. We've been looking at this all wrong. Jon doesn't want to silence Eden because of Lindsay but wants revenge because Eden helped Julie, his wife, leave him. What if I'm already too late?"

Sam gave him a censuring look. "Don't borrow trouble. We don't know anything yet. I'll meet you there."

Zach nodded and his hands shook as he climbed into the driver's seat. He gripped the steering wheel and bowed his head. "Please, Lord. Keep them safe. Keep my family safe."

Heart thudding with terror, Zach started the engine and put the vehicle in gear. In a spray of gravel, he headed out of the parking lot. Halfway to Willow Creek, his phone rang. His heart leaped. But a glance at the caller ID dashed his hope that it was Eden. He pushed the answer button. "Hey, Lucy. I've got an emergency."

"Is it Eden?" A thread of alarm ran through Lucy's tone.

His breath hitched. "How did you know?"

"I got a strange text from her," Lucy said. She sounded like she was moving fast. "She and her dad were meeting some woman at a trailhead. She couldn't find her dad and was worried."

Smart of Eden to text Lucy. Respect and admiration crowded in next to the fear filling his chest, even as dread pinched his lungs. Karl Schaffer wouldn't voluntarily leave his daughter alone. "I received the message over an hour ago saying she was going to Willow Creek Trail. I'm worried. How long ago did your message come in?"

"It just came through," Lucy said. "West and I were out searching for the illegal weapon's cachet near Pactola Lake," Lucy continued. "No cell reception out in the woods."

"Did you find anything?"

"No. But there's a lot of ground to cover. The Black Hills National Forest is huge," she said. He heard the ding of a car door opening. "But I'm headed to Willow Creek trailhead now. West is going to follow in his car and has called for backup."

"Can you have Cheyenne access Eden's phone? Julie Fielding either texted or called her asking for the meeting. And if it wasn't Julie, then it could have been her husband."

"Will do," Lucy said and hung up.

Zach stepped on the gas. From her compartment, Amber barked as if to urge him to get to Eden faster. He would move heaven and earth to do just that.

The dusty thin trail leading from the trailhead through the expanse of tall pines toward the creek and waterfall of Willow Creek started with an uphill climb. Eden chose her steps carefully. The last thing she wanted was to twist her ankle while keeping an alert eye out for any signs of her father or Julie. She couldn't be that far behind them. The dachshund with her pink collar had disappeared into the denser tree line farther up the trail.

Eden stopped to wipe the sweat from her brow. Distress crept into her chest. Where was Julie? Where was her dad? Why would her dad leave her?

He wouldn't. Something bad had to have happened to him. But how could someone have taken him away from the area without her hearing? Her dad was a big guy. It would take an equally big person to subdue him. An image of the man who'd killed Lindsay flashed through her mind. The killer had been big. Strong, if the way he and Zach had fought was any indication.

Scared to her core of losing her father on top of everything else, Eden's heart rate skyrocketed. Did she dare keep going? The trail would end at the creek. This time of year it would be swollen and rushing quickly with snowmelt from the mountains to the north. She stepped over a fallen log in the path and headed into the tree line.

"Dad? Julie?" she called out, her voice echoing through the trees.

Maybe they weren't even here. But she hadn't heard a vehicle drive up or drive away when she was in the restroom. Where could her dad be? She pulled out her phone, noting she had one bar. Not great but she could try. She pressed the button to call Zach. With the phone to her ear, she waited. There was only silence on the other end of the line. Then the call beeped. A glance at the screen showed the call failed.

She needed to turn back and call for help. If Zach wasn't available, she would call Sam. Or Lucy.

She turned around.

A shadow loomed over her.

With a gasp, she spun and found herself facing a tall, dark-haired man dressed in a leather bomber.

Jon Fielding.

She recognized her neighbor, as well as the jacket he wore. But the blond hair was missing. He'd been wearing a wig and mirrored sunglasses that hid his dark eyes. Her gaze jumped to the round barrel of a nasty-looking gun in his hand.

* * *

Zach's SUV skidded to a halt in the parking lot of the Willow Creek trailhead located off the highway west of Mount Rushmore.

Karl Schaffer's pickup truck was parked near the restroom facilities.

Zach jumped out of the vehicle and released Amber. Within moments, several other cars pulled to a stop near where Zach had haphazardly parked. Lucy Lopez burst out of her vehicle and quickly released Piper from her compartment. The springer spaniel danced around Lucy as they raced over.

West Cole halted his Plains City cruiser behind Zach's. He and his K-9, Peanut, hustled over, the beagle's legs moving fast and his ears flapping.

Sam's car screeched to a halt, and he exited the cruiser and strode at a fast clip to where Zach and the others gathered, just as another Plains City police cruiser arrived.

A tall, red-haired female patrol officer stepped out of the car. Zach wasn't surprised West had called his fiancée, Trish McCord. They had been a couple for over two months now after having worked together on a case.

"What do we know?" Sam said.

"That's Karl's truck." Zach gestured to the large silver pickup.

"We'll check the restroom," Lucy volunteered.

She and Piper hurried toward the outbuilding and disappeared inside the women's room.

Zach's gaze went to the trail marker and to the ground at the beginning of the incline. The dirt scuff marks showed activity. "Karl and Eden must've gone up the trail looking for Julie."

"Can Amber pick up their scents?" Sam asked.

"Yes. She should be able to catch their scent easily." Zach led Amber over to the truck. It was unlocked. Unusual for the former sheriff to leave his vehicle unsecured. Zach opened the cab door and motioned for Amber to jump in. She sniffed around the interior. The black Lab's tail wagged profusely at the familiar scent of Eden and Karl.

When Amber jumped back out, her paws hitting the ground soundlessly, her nose lifted in the air. Her black ears twitched and then her snout went to the ground.

"She has one of their scents," Zach muttered, his heartbeat in his throat. Where was his wife? What happened to her father?

Amber's body quivered as she tracked an odor along the ground. Her tail stood up and her ears lay almost flat against her dark head as she approached a picnic table near the restrooms. She sniffed all around the table, lifted her nose in the air, and then back to the ground, recapturing the scent. She skirted the table and shuffled along the ground, around behind the facilities building to a large metal trash container. She sat, her tongue rolling to the side and her dark eyes stared fixedly at the garbage receptacle. She was alerting. Zach's heart plummeted.

"Oh, Lord. Please no." Zach's muttered prayer filled his ears, but was quickly replaced by the roar of his blood rushing to his head. He exchanged a grim glance with West. They approached the dumpster, each taking an end of the large metal lid and flipping it backward, exposing the interior of the container. Zach held his breath, more out of fear of what he was about to find than from the putrid assault to his senses as he peered over the metal edge into the dark garbage-filled interior.

Karl Schaffer lay on top of black garbage bags. Duct tape covered his mouth. Zip ties held his hands and feet together. His eyes were closed.

Fearful for Karl's safety, Zach, Sam and West lifted Karl out of the dumpster. He had a bloody gash on the back of his head.

They laid him on top of the picnic table.

Sam pressed his fingers against Karl's neck. "He's alive."

Trish rushed over with a first aid kit. She snapped open reviving salts and put them under Karl's nose.

Lucy and Piper stood nearby, with Lucy on the phone.

Karl regained consciousness with a jolt. His eyes fluttered open as he thrashed about on the table. His plaid shirt was stained dark red from the blood loss from the head wound. Trish quickly ripped open a sterile gauze pad and pressed it to the injury.

Zach put his hands on his shoulders. "Settle. You're safe."

Karl's eyes practically bugged out of his head. He tried to speak, but his words were muffled by the tape covering his mouth.

"This is going to hurt." Zach picked up the edge of the duct tape, lifting a corner.

Karl nodded.

With a quick movement, Zach ripped the tape from Karl's mouth along with a couple layers of skin.

Sam clipped the zip ties, freeing Karl's hands and feet.

Karl sat up. "Where's Eden?"

"We don't know," Zach said. "Tell us what happened."

"She went into the restroom to look for her friend Julie." Karl swung his legs over the side of the table. "I was sitting here on the table when something hard hit me on the back of the head, and that's the last thing I remember."

"There's a message written on the mirror in lipstick inside the women's restroom," Lucy supplied. "It says 'Headed up trail.' And it's signed with a J. Also, I just received a call from Cheyenne. The call that came into Eden's phone was from a burner."

"Then that's what we do," Zach said. "Let's get to work. We have to find my wife."

Wishing he hadn't returned Eden's scarf to her, Zach hunched down so that he was at eye level with Amber. "I need your super smeller. We have to find Eden."

At the mention of Eden's name, Amber perked up. She barked, her whole body quivering with renewed energy.

Letting Amber have the full length of the lead, Zach cast her toward the trail. "Find Eden."

The dog's nose went to the ground and she took off. Zach and the others followed, and with every step, Zach prayed they found his wife before something happened to her and their child.

SIXTEEN

The confusion running through Eden's system barely matched the panic gripping her in a tight vice. Her steps slowed.

Finding herself face-to-face with Jon Fielding holding a gun on her in the middle of the Willow Creek Trail had been the furthest thing she'd expected. But she should have guessed after Amber led Zach to the Fieldings' home.

Jon had confiscated her phone and then forced her to keep heading up the trail toward the creek.

"Keep moving," Jon said, with a nudge at her back.

"What did you do to my father?" Eden's voice broke as she picked up the pace. Was her dad lying somewhere bleeding, perhaps dying? Despair threatened to render her unable to function.

"You should be more concerned for yourself," Jon said.

"Is Julie even here?" Had he already killed her? Why did Jon want to hurt Eden?

"Oh, she's here." Anger reverberated through his voice. "I made sure of that."

Eden fisted her hands in an effort to stem the terror racing through her. "Is she alive?"

"Yes. Unfortunately."

Not dead. A relief. "She's the one who texted me?"

"No. I did that. And I texted her pretending to be you asking her to meet you here," he said. "But that dreaded dog of hers distracted me just enough to allow Julie to escape and run into the trees. But she's not far. I can feel her."

Julie was alive and somewhere in the forest. Eden sent up a prayer that Julie had a way to call for help. Maybe she would double back and flag down a car on the highway.

"Why did you lure me here?"

"Because all of this is your fault. No one makes a fool of me without consequences."

His tone took on a petulance that made Eden wince. "My fault?"

"If you hadn't talked my wife into leaving me, none of this would be happening," he said. "But you did. No one else would put up with the things I've had to deal with from her. I'm the only one who will take care of her. She's nothing without me. She'll learn, though. Just as Lindsay did."

Eden sucked in a sharp breath. "You did kill Lindsay." Having her suspicion confirmed wasn't gratifying. She glanced over her shoulder at him. "You wore a wig. And glasses."

Jon's mouth twisted in a sneer. "That's right. But you saw me. I couldn't have you identifying me. And then I realized who you were…it was as if the universe was handing me my revenge on a platter."

"I honestly didn't know it was you until just now," she replied. "You should have just left town."

"Leave?" He scoffed. "I'm not the one who should be made to give up their life. I've worked hard for what I have. If Julie had just done as she was told and not made a fuss over Lindsay, then none of this would have happened."

Jon and Lindsay? "You and Lindsay were having an affair?" Eden couldn't imagine the young ranger being interested in Jon. But then again, Lindsay had been seeing Pat Dunbar, who was also quite a bit older than her.

"We were, but she called it off because Julie got to her," Jon said. "Nobody leaves me and gets away with it."

There was a rustling off to the right, drawing their attention. Lightning fast, Jon lunged forward, wrapping an arm around Eden's waist and drawing her back against his chest. He put the gun to her temple.

A shiver of fear ran over Eden.

"Julie," Jon intoned in a commanding voice.

"Come out. Or I'll kill your friend. And her death will be on your head."

"No!" Eden shouted. "Run for help."

From her peripheral vision, Eden saw Jon lift his hand a second before the butt of the gun connected to the side of her head. Bright lights and pain exploded behind her eyes and her knees gave out. But Jon's strong arm around her waist held her upright. Struggling to remain conscious, her chin slumped to her chest. She closed her eyes against the pounding in her head from the blow.

"Don't hurt her." Julie's voice came from somewhere to Eden's right.

Eden forced her eyes open enough to see the thicket of bushes Julie must be hiding within. Eden wanted to again urge Julie to run, but her head simply hurt too much.

"Show yourself," Jon shouted.

Recalling the self-defense training her father and Zach had both imparted to her, Eden relaxed her body completely, forcing Jon to take more of her weight. She couldn't let Julie emerge from the thicket. Jon would shoot her. And then he would shoot Eden. He would kill her and Zach's child. She couldn't let that happen. She wouldn't.

Taking a breath and calming her mind, she gritted her teeth against the pain and exploded into action. She flung her head back, hitting Jon in the chest. At the same moment, she stomped down hard with her foot on his instep and used the heel of her hand to drive into his groin.

He gave a guttural shout of pain and released his hold across her waist. She wrenched his thumb back and pushed his arm away before sweeping her leg in an arc and kicking his feet out from beneath him. She didn't wait to see him drop. She took off running for the thicket.

Jon let out an angry yell.

Eden dove for Julie, who crouched behind a clump of bushes, taking her to the ground, just as shots rang out.

The bullets went through the thicket and embedded in a nearby tree.

"We have to get out of here," Eden said to a wide-eyed Julie. "Stay low. We have to run."

Taking inspiration from her husband and remembering what he'd said about never running in a straight line when being shot at, Eden, with Julie at her heels, ran in a crouched, zigzag pattern deeper into the forest.

Gunfire in the distance echoed through the forest, the reverberations scattering birds from branches. The high-pitched cry of a bald eagle filled the air as the bird soared overhead. Zach's heart jammed into his throat. Urgency, born of panic and fear, urged him to move faster, which in turn caused Amber to speed up, nearly dragging Zach.

Abruptly, the black Lab jerked to the right, charged off into the bushes left of the trail and headed into the trees. The thick underbrush slapped at Zach's legs as he maneuvered through the dense foliage.

"Find Eden," Zach urged between pants for breath. His mounting terror made the air seem too thick to draw fully into his lungs.

Amber raced to a thicket of low-growing shrubs and dried branches. The earth was disturbed around the tangle of plants and debris, indicating someone had been there. Eden? Suddenly, his brain swirled with questions. Had she used the vegetation as cover? Where had she gone? Why did Jon Fielding want her dead? Was he the man who killed Lindsay Nash? If so, why? They hadn't found a connection between the two. The pieces of the puzzle weren't fitting together.

Zach wouldn't know the whole picture until they found Eden and took Jon into custody. And he would find Eden. He refused to accept an alternative.

Amber picked up a scent, her long thin tail pinging up and her ears flattening back on her broad head as she zigzagged a swath through the tall ponderosa and spruce trees. The carpet of needles beneath their feet quieted their steps.

Regret over the time he'd allowed to pass while he'd given his fear free rein to rule his actions, keeping him from Eden's side, pounded at Zach's head like an anvil. He couldn't contemplate the past now. He had to concentrate on the present, the need to keep moving, to find his wife and child.

The roar of the waterfall created by Willow Creek drowned out Eden's breathing. She and Julie needed to get to the other side of the swollen creek. If they could head toward Mount Rushmore National Memorial, they could get to the safety of the ranger's station. Beside her, Julie stumbled and fell to her knees. It took precious moments to get her back onto her feet.

Supporting Julie with an arm around her waist, Eden urged her to move.

"We have to cross the creek," Eden told her as they neared the rushing water.

"How deep is it?" Julie shoved her tangled dark hair from her dirt-streaked face. Soil and pine needles from the towering ponderosa's clung to her clothing.

"Can't be more than waist high. You'll be fine." Eden cringed at the irritation in her tone. Taking her anger and fear out on Julie wasn't productive. Eden needed to keep her head if she wanted to make it out of this situation alive. She was a trained park ranger. Granted, most of her career had been limited to the confines of Mount Rushmore National Memorial, but she'd taken wilderness survival training classes and had boondocked in the forest multiple times.

But she'd never been pursued through the forest by a man bent on killing her.

At the water's edge, Julie hesitated. "It looks cold."

Biting the inside of her lip, Eden didn't comment as she plunged into the water without taking off her sneakers. The shoes would keep her feet from being cut on rocks or other debris. Not to mention removing them would waste precious time.

The icy creek water sent shivers through Eden's body, but she tried to keep her voice from quavering. "Come on," Eden urged. "We have to get to the other side."

Julie moved slowly into the water with a gasp. Eden held out her hand and guided the woman through the creek. Water rushed around their knees as they trudged forward.

The creek bed slanted at a sharp downward angle and they dropped down to their waists.

Eden hissed as her stomach muscles contracted with shock. She sent up a prayer that the chill wouldn't harm the baby she carried.

Julie let out a gasp of surprise. "I'm going to freeze."

"Keep moving!" Eden encouraged.

The going was slow, each step an effort as her core temperature dropped. Below the water's surface, the earth rose and became shallow again and they reach the bank of the creek.

Julie stood shivering and panting. "N-now wh-what?"

From the other side of the creek where they'd just come, the noise of Jon running toward them sounded like thunder.

Grabbing Julie's hand, Eden practically had to drag the woman through the trees. Her soggy clothes attracted clumps of needles, dirt and leaves. Water sloshed through her sneakers. She could feel a blister forming. But she assumed a blister hurt far less than a potential bullet wound.

The terrain became steeper as they moved up a hill toward one of the many limestone formations that jutted out of the ground throughout the Black Hills. Beside her, Julie huffed and her movements were jerky. She didn't think Julie could be able to go much farther.

Pausing to assess, Eden saw an opening in the rock where wind, water and no doubt human activity had created a cave.

"Head for that cutout." Eden pointed to the nearest opening.

Julie nodded and seemed more invigorated to have a destination in sight and greatly increased her speed. Later, Eden would tell her how good a job she was doing. But for now, Eden's focus was on getting inside the cave and hoping that

Jon would pass by them, unaware of where they were hiding.

Eden slowed as the loose rock beneath her feet shifted and slid down behind her. Scrambling side by side, they made it to the small ledge at the mouth of the cave. Desperate for the cover the opening provided, they rushed into the darkness. The air stank and felt thick in Eden's nose. Obviously, some animal used the cave as a home. And Eden had a strong sense they weren't alone. A tremor worked over her flesh. The wet clothes clinging to her made her skin numb.

A shuffling sound at the back of the cave raised the hairs on Eden's arms.

"What is that?" Julie's panicked voice echoed through the cavernous cave.

"I don't know," Eden answered honestly with trepidation tripping over her tongue. There were any number of creatures that could be using the cave as a habitat. Bears, goats, cougars and coyotes.

Any of which wouldn't be happy to find her and Julie invading their space.

She groped in the dark for Julie and snagged her arm, pulling her toward the cave's rough wall. Dropping her voice to a whisper, she said, "We just have to give Jon time enough to pass by then we can leave."

Somewhere outside the cave came the plaintive barks of Julie's dachshund. Had the dog crossed the creek? Eden couldn't tell how far away the barks were coming from. Did dachshunds even know how to swim? Or was it caught somewhere with its leash tangled around a tree?

"Sweet Pea," Julie exclaimed and rushed past Eden.

"Wait!" Eden whisper-shouted, but it was too late. Julie left the safety of the cave to scramble down the hill in search of her beloved pet.

Moments later the loud retort of a gun bounced off the cave walls. Eden ran to the mouth of the cave and peered out in time to see Julie dive to the left behind a large boulder. Jon, dripping wet and clearly agitated, aimed at the rock and fired, sending bits and pieces of the granite flying.

Picking up a rock from the floor of the cave, Eden heaved off to the side, hoping to give Julie an opportunity to escape and find help. Jon whirled around and fired in the direction Eden had thrown the rock. Julie darted away, disappearing into the forest.

Jon lifted his gaze toward the cave. Quickly, Eden ducked away from the mouth of the cave, praying for help.

From the black depths of the cavern, a loud snorting noise jolted through her. Gasping at the unexpected sound, her hand went to her heart as she recognized the warning grunts and huffing.

She was trapped in the dark with a wild mountain goat.

SEVENTEEN

More gunfire rang out. Closer. Fearing for Eden, Zach pressed forward, pushing himself to the brink of his endurance. He could hear the others behind him, trying to keep up. The seconds ticked by like hours as he and Amber raced through the forest toward where the shots had come from.

Up ahead, something crashed through the underbrush, coming straight for them.

Zach held up a hand. The others behind him stopped and fanned out.

Hope flared. *Please, let it be Eden*, Zach lifted up the prayer.

A dark-haired woman carrying a brown smooth-coated dachshund, sporting a pink collar and dragging a pink leash, burst out from behind a clump of trees.

Julie Fielding. She was soaking wet from the waist down. When she saw Zach, she fell to her knees, released the dog, who took off running past Zach, and covered her face with her hands.

Zach rushed to her side and gripped her shoulders. "Where's Eden?"

"Jon has her trapped in a cave on the other side of the creek," Julie managed between hiccupping sobs.

The others gathered around. Lucy held the dachshund's leash along with Piper's lead.

"We have to proceed with caution," Zach said to Sam, West and Lucy. "But if it's a choice between Eden or Jon, I'll take the shot." Though it was every law enforcement officer's objective to minimize injury to everyone involved, Zach wouldn't hesitate if it meant keeping Eden safe.

"Without question," Sam said.

"Agreed," West said. "I'll radio Trish and let her know we need more assistance."

"I'll stay with Julie," Lucy said. Beside her, Piper sniffed at the woman but lost interest and began sniffing at the ground. Lucy reeled the springer spaniel close. Julie picked up her dog and held her against her chest.

Zach was grateful to the Fargo officer. "I appreciate it."

With renewed determination, Zach hurried forward. He would save Eden if it was the last thing he did.

With Amber leading the race, Zach, Sam and West, with his beagle, Peanut, made it to the creek. The water flowed past in a swirling rush. Without hesitation, West picked up Peanut, cradled the dog under his arm and waded into the creek.

Zach grabbed the handle on the top of Amber's harness to make sure she didn't lose her footing as they charged into the chilly water. He kept her close to his body while still giving the black Lab room to swim when the water deepened. Sam forged a path across unencumbered.

Once they reached the other side of the creek, Amber shook, spraying water in every direction. The cold didn't seem to bother the dog. Her sleek, wet black coat gleamed in the sunshine. Zach ignored the squishing water inside his heavy boots as he headed toward the caves dug out in the side of the hill. He and Eden had taken this trail numerous times.

They usually stopped at the creek and turned back. But on several occasions when Zach and Amber had come here on their own, they'd crossed the creek and explored the granite and limestone rocks jutting up from the ground. He'd seen the cutouts in the sides of the rocks and had seen a cougar nearby. He could only hope and pray that Jon Fielding was their only predator today.

When they were in view of the cave, Zach's heart pitched. Jon Fielding stood on the ledge outside the opening. Zach quickly motioned for Sam and West to take cover with him behind a large boulder that appeared to have pockmarks from bullets. The three of them hunched down with the dogs.

"You two spread out," Zach directed. "We need to surround him. I'll draw him away from the opening."

Sam nodded. "Careful. The guy's squirrely."

"I'm prepared to do what I need to," Zach said. He turned to Amber and gave her the signal for down. The dog folded her legs beneath her but was situated so that she could easily spring to life at a moment's notice. Zach said in a whisper to her, "Stay. Eyes on me."

The dog's beautiful amber eyes held his. She would obey and be ready when he needed her.

In a crouch, Zach ran forward until he could take cover behind the thick trunk of a towering ponderosa pine tree. Jon was maybe fifty feet away now. He'd climbed to the small ledge of the cave and stood there muttering to himself and waving the gun in the air.

Withdrawing his holstered weapon, Zach stepped out from behind the boulder and called out, "Jon Fielding, put the gun down."

Without complying, Jon raced inside the dark cavern.

Frustration had Zach clenching his fists. "Jon, there's nowhere for you to go. If you don't come out now, we will come in after you."

A strange noise emanated from the cave followed by a single gunshot and a scream.

Terror struck Zach through the heart.

"No!" he shouted, fearing that the man had just killed his family.

Covering her ringing ears, Eden crouched in the dark. After hearing her husband's voice, she'd seen Jon run into the cave and had seen the way he'd jolted with surprise and screamed when the goat had let out a protest at yet another intruder. She hadn't expected Jon to fire blindly at the beast.

Thankfully, the bullet hadn't hit her or the animal.

She couldn't discern where Jon was now in the darkness.

Where was Zach? He'd come for her. Her heart thrummed with joy and fear and everything in between.

Did she dare make a break for the cave entrance? She inched her way along the wall toward the entrance, deciding it was worth the risk. Just as she pushed away from the wall and ran toward the mouth of the cave, Jon snatched her by the hair and pulled her back against him.

She clawed at his hands.

He pushed the barrel of the gun into her kidneys. "Don't think I won't shoot you. I know you're pregnant. That's what you were doing at the obstetrician clinic."

Stilling, she closed her eyes with fresh fear and lifted a prayer that God would protect her and the baby.

Zach needed time to rescue her. She had every confidence that her husband would do so. He was that kind of man. She'd known it when she'd fallen in love with him on their second date. And she still loved him.

If she got out of this situation alive, she was going to tell him. There was no way she could let her pride and hurt keep her and the baby from the man they both needed.

Holding on to her hair with one hand and keeping the gun pressed to her kidneys with the other, Jon pushed her forward until they stood at the opening of the cave.

Eden blinked at the brightness of the sunlight. When she managed to clear the stinging from her eyes, her husband came into view. Her heart bumped against her ribs at the sight. His uniform dripped with creek water, and dirt, needles and leaves clung to him as they did her, but he'd never looked more handsome.

He was alone. Where was Amber? She glanced around, not seeing his K-9 or anyone else.

"You'll let me pass, or I'll kill her," Jon shouted. "I've got nothing left to lose."

Eden closed her eyes. She, on the other hand, had everything to lose.

* * *

Zach reined in the fury engulfing him as he stared up at Jon Fielding, who held a gun pressed to Zach's wife's back and gripped her hair in his fist. They stood on the small ledge in front of the cave that had been carved out of the rock jutting up out of the ground. He thought he'd known terror but this—

I've got nothing left to lose.

Her captor's words reverberated through Zach, pounding at his head. Jon Fielding had already killed once and would no doubt do so again if given the opportunity. Zach couldn't let that happen. Not to Eden.

What were his choices? Anything he did now put Eden at risk. Even complying. There was no guarantee Jon wouldn't make good his threat.

After holstering his weapon, Zach held out his hands to the side. He prayed with all his might that Jon wouldn't realize that with just hand motions Zach could activate and direct Amber.

Too many times they'd been on calls responding to a report of a person in distress. Zach would keep the person talking while Amber moved, getting closer until she could latch on to the person and drag them away from whatever ledge, cliff or crevice the person threatened to throw themselves off.

"You may not have anything to lose, Jon, but I

do," Zach said. "I will not draw my gun on you. Let Eden go and you can walk away."

"I don't believe you," Jon shouted.

Zach gestured with his left hand while keeping his right palm facing up toward Jon. He stepped to the side, drawing Jon's attention away from where Amber now crept out from behind the boulder. The black Lab's head and body were in a near crouch as she moved slowly toward her target. Her amber-colored eyes darted from Jon to Zach to check that she was doing as he wanted.

"Jon, I understand you're upset." Zach took a few more steps to the right. Jon shifted to follow him as Zach had hoped he would. Amber advanced up the hill toward the cave. "Julie left you. Maybe with some counseling you two could work things out."

"That's a nice thought," Jon yelled. "But we're done. And I'll never be free. Julie and this woman have to pay."

Zach thought about that statement. "Why were you arguing with Lindsay Nash in Mount Rushmore?"

Jon waved the gun in the air, and Zach let out a slow, relieved breath that it was no longer positioned at Eden's back.

"That ingrate. She wouldn't take me back after Julie left me," Jon said. "She said she'd found someone else. It's all Julie's fault. Julie confronted her last year. Julie said she and I could make it work but she lied." The gun was again aimed at Eden's back. "And then this one interfered. She convinced Julie to leave me. And she saw me with Lindsay. Saw what Lindsay made me do. Women need to be put in their place."

Zach met Eden's gaze. The fear in her green eyes gutted him. He needed to find a way to de-escalate the situation. He needed to find a way to keep Eden safe.

Inches away from the edge of the ledge that had been carved out of the stone rock, jutting a good ten feet from the hard-packed dirt below, Eden's heart pumped so rapidly she was surprised her ribs managed to keep the muscle inside of her body. Her bruised eardrums from the gunfire made the world sound muffled.

She glanced around, searching through the trees, trying to see Zach's backup. She wanted to believe that Lucy and Sam would have her husband's back. That they would have her back.

Where was Amber? Wherever Zach was the dog was not far away. She recalled tales of Zach and Amber's heroic rescues and took heart, knowing that somewhere Amber was positioned to take Jon down. But would it be in time?

Another noisy snort from inside the cave caused Eden to jerk and step forward.

Jon whirled around, facing the cave. "What is that thing?"

Before Eden could tell him it was one of the hundreds of wild mountain goats that roamed the Black Hills National Forest since the 1920s, another sound filled her with dread.

Hooves striking stone echoed through the cave. The earth shook.

A large white mountain goat, with matted fur and slender black horns that curved slightly back toward its head, charged out of the cave.

Jon screamed and released his hold on Eden.

With momentum, the goat rammed his pointed horns into Jon's torso and flipped him upward, sending him head over heels through the air. He landed with a thud and a bounce on the hill below the cave. Blood seeped from where he'd been gored.

Lowering its head, the mountain goat turned toward Eden.

Breath jamming in her throat, she put up her hands. "Whoa!"

A blur of black caught Eden's focus as Amber streaked up the hill, leaping onto the short ledge and planting herself between the goat and Eden.

Amber's deep growl permeated the air.

With a loud series of grunts and snorts, the mountain goat reared on its hind legs and lowered its horns toward Amber. The dog backed up, bumping into Eden. Startled, Eden stumbled over the slight ledge, falling toward the hillside. She braced herself for impact when strong arms caught her. She met her rescuer's gaze and found herself staring into the warm brown eyes of her husband.

The mountain goat dropped to all fours and veered away from Amber to scramble up the side of the rock face, and with ease it climbed out of reach.

Amber whined as she watched the goat crest the top of the rock and disappear. Clearly, the dog wanted to chase after the beast.

"Come," Zach instructed his partner.

Without hesitation, Amber leaped off the ledge and moved to Zach's side.

From out of the forest, West and Sam rushed to check on Jon, who lay unmoving where he'd landed. West's K-9 sniffed Jon before losing interest. The beagle sat and watched as Sam checked Jon's neck for a pulse.

"He's alive," Sam said. "We need to get paramedics here to carry him out."

A fresh wave of panic hit her. "Jon did something to my father," she told Zach.

"He's safe," Zach said, tightening his hold on her. "We found him."

Tension left her body. Her father was alive. She wrapped her arms around Zach's neck.

Zach turned and moved, his strong long legs eating up the ground as he carried her away from the horrible scene.

A sense of déjà vu hit her. "You don't need to carry me. I can walk."

He arched an eyebrow. "I want to."

Deciding she would allow it, for now, she held on. When they reached the creek, and she realized he intended to walk into the creek with her in his arms, she said, "Put me down. Now."

"Can you make it across?" Zach peered at her with worry.

"I made it across once, I can do it again," she told him.

With apparent reluctance, he set her on her feet.

She waded into the icy water, eager to get to the other side and away from this place. She would never think about the forest the same way. She hated that Jon had ruined a place once so dear to her.

Zach grabbed the handle on Amber's tracking harness and helped her cross the flowing creek. When they were on the other side, Zach made a move toward picking Eden up again, but she darted away. As much as she appreciated his gallant effort, it made her feel like a wimp to be carried around like a victim.

"I can walk from here," she told him. They met up with Lucy, her English springer spaniel, Piper, and Julie and little Sweet Pea. The short-legged, long-bodied dog seemed captivated by the springer spaniel.

Julie squealed and rushed to hug Eden. "I was so worried."

Extracting herself, Eden said, "You did good, Julie." To Lucy, Eden said, "You got my message."

"I did once we came out of the woods," Lucy said. Piper seemed distracted, wanting to follow a scent. "Sorry, it took us so long to get here. We were out in another area doing a search."

Though Lucy didn't specify what they'd been searching for, Eden knew from Zach that the task force had been covering all of the national forest parks in the area looking for supposed buried illegal weapons.

"We're all safe," Eden said. "That's what matters."

Julie fell into step beside Eden and Zach. Amber walked ahead of them down the incline of the Willow Creek Trail. They reached the trailhead parking lot, where an ambulance and several police cars waited. Another ambulance arrived, and two paramedics rushed up the trail with Lucy and Piper as their guide.

Eden's gaze zeroed in on her father, and she rushed to his side where he sat on the back of the ambulance bumper.

A bandage around his head gave her pause. "Are you okay?"

"Peachy now that I see you," her father said and opened his arms for a hug.

She moved into his embrace and breathed in the rancid odor clinging to his clothes. She drew back with a grimace. "What happened? You stink."

Karl scoffed. "I'm getting old. The punk snuck up on me. I took a blow to the head and ended up in the garbage bin. But Amber found me."

Eden sent up a prayer of thanks for the dog's keen sense of smell. How she discerned her father's scent from the stench of garbage Eden couldn't fathom. Her gaze went to where Zach and Amber were talking with several other officers and deputies.

The paramedic handed Eden a bottle of water. She drank from it as she and her father waited for Jon Fielding to be brought out from the forest. It wasn't long before Lucy with Piper, West with his dog, Peanut, and Sam returned with Jon strapped to a litter carried by two paramedics. They put a still unconscious Jon into the back of the second ambulance. Sam climbed inside the back bay to escort Jon to the hospital.

Eden breathed a sigh of relief.

Zach conferred with Lucy and West before the two took their dogs and headed back up the Willow Creek Trail.

"Excuse me, Dad," Eden said and hurried to Zach, where he stood watching his fellow task force members.

"Where are they going?"

Zach faced her. "Both dogs caught a scent near the creek."

She knew the specialty of the two dogs. Both were trained to detect weapons and explosives respectively. "Go with Lucy and West. I'm safe now. I'm going with my father to the hospital."

Zach frowned. "They can handle it."

Eden put her hand over his heart. "You're a team. Go do your job." Seeing the protest on his face, she added, "I need space."

Though it hurt her to say the words, she knew she was doing the right thing.

Zach grimaced and emotions filled his eyes. But there wasn't time. She needed to go with her father.

She needed to think.

Because some way, somehow, she was going to repair her marriage and get to the bottom of why Zach didn't feel he could be a parent.

EIGHTEEN

Zach watched the ambulance containing Eden and her father drive away. She'd told him she needed space. Space to think about their future. A future without him? A heaviness settled on his shoulders. How had it come to this?

His fault. Again. Fear had a stranglehold on him. Fear of the future. Fear of failure.

At least, Jon Fielding was no longer a threat to Eden.

Zach would take solace in knowing he'd put an end to the danger and his wife was safe.

He and Amber hustled to catch up to West and Lucy and their dogs. They kept a good pace up the trail to the spot where Peanut and Piper both began tracking a trail away from the creek and from the cave where Eden had been held hostage. Amber trotted along with the other dogs, as if curious about what trail they were following.

The dogs led Zach and the others to a recently disturbed mound that had been covered with dried leaves and branches. Peanut sat, waiting.

West pulled the little beagle back and gave her a treat.

Piper sat, as well, and stared at the mound.

Zach knew both dogs were trained in a passive alert as a safeguard in case whatever they found was volatile. "Good dog," Lucy said and offered a reward to Piper.

Amber stood watching, her head cocked. Then she turned her amber-colored eyes to Zach as if to say "where's mine?" Zach chuckled and handed over a small treat.

"There's something buried there," Lucy said. "I brought a shovel." From the backpack she wore she produced a folding metal shovel. West also had a similar shovel in his pack.

They began digging. Zach jumped in and they took turns. Zach's shovel hit something metal.

They dug quicker around the sides of a long metal lockbox. They dragged it out of the hole. West popped open the lid, and they found at least six rifles with bump stocks, several handguns and a half dozen flash-bangs.

"This is a win," West said. "Hopefully, we can find evidence on this box and these weapons to lead us to this Brandon person or someone else that can help us bring down this gun trafficking ring."

"I'll radio the boss," Lucy said. "He may decide to stake out the area and see who returns for these weapons."

Zach thought about Eden at the hospital. About her need for space. Maybe he needed to volunteer to be the one to stake out the illegal weapons cachet spot.

Once Lucy had Daniel on the radio, she told him about the metal box with the weapons inside.

"That's great. I'll send reinforcement." Daniel's voice crackled over the radio. "Is Zach with you?"

Zach stepped forward. "Here. This is quite the haul."

"You need to get to the hospital," Daniel said.

Zach's heart stalled out. "What's happened?"

"Jon Fielding escaped police custody."

Eden sat beside her father's bed holding his hand. He had a mild concussion. The doctor said he would be able to leave in a few hours. They were just running some additional blood work to make sure everything was as it should be.

Sam Powell burst into the room. His eye was swollen, and his jaw sported what looked like the beginning of a horrible bruise. "You good?"

"From the looks of it, I'm doing better than you are," she said, rising from the chair. "Who did that to your face?"

"Jon Fielding."

Terror struck Eden. "What?"

Sam grimaced then winced, no doubt from pain. "He must've been pretending to be unconscious. As soon as we arrived in the ambulance bay, I hopped out to speak with the staff and he clocked the other paramedic with an oxygen tank. Then I tried to subdue him, but he landed a well-placed right hook, and I went down just long enough to allow him to escape. I wanted to make sure he didn't come looking for you."

Eden stumbled back into the chair.

"He's a sneaky one," Karl said from the bed. "Next time you guys get him, you have to put a straitjacket on him. Something he can't get out of."

Sam nodded. "Zach's on his way. I've stationed guards outside your door."

"Thank you." Stunned, Eden watched Sam leave the room. She couldn't believe this wasn't over. Would the man never stop? Maybe this time he would actually leave town and realize he wasn't going to be able to get to her or his wife, Julie. Lucy had arranged for Julie to leave town for a safe place out of state.

Dad's hand on her arm drew her attention.

"Have you and Zach talked?"

She grimaced. "Not yet. But as soon as we get you home, we will."

"Good. I didn't like thinking about something happening to you and the baby," Karl said. "I can only imagine how upsetting it was for Zach. Give him a chance. And remember that you married Zach for a reason."

There wasn't just one reason why she'd married

Zach. There had been a whole host of reasons. All of them were as true today as they had been the day she decided to say yes when he proposed. Now, she only needed to convince him to trust her enough, love her enough and love their baby enough to get past whatever it was that was keeping him from embracing the family they were meant to be. But with Jon Fielding having escaped and still at large, she could only pray they survived long enough to have a chance.

An hour later Zach, Lucy and West and their respective dogs all arrived at the hospital. Zach was grateful to his friends for the backup. He scrutinized each person he came across as he made his way through the hospital. With Jon on the loose, Zach couldn't be too careful. He was even more grateful to find Eden and her father safe, both of them resting. And a guard outside their door. After a quick conversation with the doctor to see if Karl was well enough to leave, to which the answer was yes, Zach went into the room. Eden was so beautiful, all curled up in the chair with her chin on her chest and lilting to the side. The way she was sleeping, she would end up with a crick in her neck.

"Honey," Zach said softly. "Wake up."

Her eyes fluttered open, and she smiled when she saw him. "Did you find anything?"

He loved that she thought to ask. But he was

more concerned with her safety. "We did. And I can tell you about it later. For now, I want to get you and your father back to his house. Lucy is going to stay with us until Jon is captured again."

Eden rose and stretched. Zach loved the way she moved. Graceful and lithe. He stepped aside so that Eden could wake her father. The discharge process went smoothly. With West and Lucy both following close behind, Zach drove Eden and her father back to the Schaffer family home with a heightened sense of alertness to every car that passed. Would Jon take advantage of his freedom and flee? Or would he try to hurt Eden again out of his need for revenge?

Once they were securely inside the Schaffer home, Zach was amused by how Eden tried to convince her father to settle in his room, but he insisted on a lounge chair on the back patio.

Moving into the kitchen where he could keep an eye on Eden through the window, Zach didn't want her out of his sight even though the others had gone outside with her and her dad. He started the prep for dinner by chopping up vegetables and lettuce to make a salad. He had four steaks set out to barbecue. He knew they all had to be famished. He was, at least. And was grateful that her father had these necessary supplies.

There was a knock on the front door that sent Piper and Amber barking as they raced to the front of the house.

Zach hoped it was Sam with an update but still the need for caution had him placing his hand on his weapon, ready to draw it as he headed out of the kitchen for the front door. He motioned Eden back when she and Lucy entered from the slider. Zach was grateful to see Lucy step in front of Eden, ready to take a bullet for her if necessary.

Keeping his hand on his sidearm, Zach opened the door, and instead of Sam, it was the elementary school librarian, Leslie Perkins.

Removing his hand from his weapon, Zach looked past the woman, noting her blue sedan car parked in the driveway. He searched for the sheriff's cruiser and saw it parked beneath a tree at the end of the drive.

"Hello," Leslie said.

"Sorry." He mentally winced at his rudeness and focused on the librarian.

The woman barely came to Zach's shoulder. She wore a blue dress that came to her ankles, and her curly hair, a vibrant shade of red, was loose and gleamed in the setting sun. She smiled. "Zach Kelcey. I'd heard you married Eden."

Zach cocked his head, totally confused as to why she would be here. "Can I help you, Mrs. Perkins?"

"Oh, please, call me Leslie," she said.

Eden nudged him aside. "Come in. Dad's out back."

Concern darkened the librarian's eyes. "One of

the nurses at the hospital called me and told me he'd been discharged. I didn't even know he was in the hospital."

"I'll let Dad tell you all about it," Eden said, tucking her arms through the woman's.

Zach gave Eden a *what's going on?* kind of look.

She just grinned and escorted Leslie out to the back patio.

When Eden returned, Zach snagged her hand and pulled her close. "What gives? The librarian?"

"Shh, she'll hear." Eden pulled him out the front door to the porch, where they settled on the porch swing in clear view of the officer sitting in his cruiser.

Thankfully, Lucy and West were tending to the barbecue.

"Dad's dating," Eden said, in a near whisper.

"I don't think they can hear us from here," Zach said. "So the librarian and the sheriff are a couple."

"Former sheriff." She frowned "I believe the librarian is still the librarian. Dad didn't say if she'd retired."

Searching her face, he asked, "How do you feel about it?"

"I was a bit stunned at first, but I'm really happy for my father. He deserves to love again." She took both of Zach's hands in hers. Her palms were smooth, her unpainted fingernails curled around his. "There's something you need to tell me, isn't there?"

His stomach dropped. Oh, no. What had she heard? "What did your father tell you?"

"Only that you have a story and that I need to hear it from you."

Grateful to the former sheriff for keeping his word that he would not reveal his past, Zach weighed his options. He could either confess to his most awful secret, or leave. He didn't think he could handle her disappointment in him.

"Do you not trust me?"

Eden's softly asked question scored him to the quick.

"Of course I trust you. I just—" He looked away from her, staring out at the tree-lined street before them. All was quiet. Twilight shadows were beginning to yawn over the yards. With a fellow deputy on duty at the end of the driveway, Eden was safe. Jon wouldn't dare show his face here.

Realizing he was stalling, he gathered his courage to face her and say, "I'm just so ashamed."

She squeezed his hands. "Tell me."

He looked away. Did he dare? Words bubbled up wanting to be set free. Would he be set free? Braving her scorn and risking the end of the most significant relationship in his life, he said, "Have you ever wondered why my sister, Caron, limps?"

When she didn't answer, he met her gaze.

There was a gentle curiosity in her pretty eyes. "She told me it was from a horse accident."

"That's so like my sister." Love for his sibling filled his chest. "Even though she's seven years younger, she's always been protective."

"The protection gene must run in your family," Eden said with a soft smile.

"Not really," he told her. "My parents were… not neglectful, but very busy. My dad with the ranch and my mom with her job at the bank. They attended lots of social and charity events, too."

"And you resented their jobs and the time away from you," she said. "I get it. When I was young, my dad was always off saving the world, or at least our little part of the world, and I was jealous that other people got to spend more time with him than me. But then my mother got sick and everything changed."

Zach nodded. He'd heard about her mother's illness, but he was just older enough that he'd already been entrenched in the state police academy when Mrs. Schaffer passed.

"When Caron and I were young, my parents left me to babysit." The words stuck in his throat. He had to give a little cough to get them to come out. "On one particular day, I was bitter and resentful to be left with my baby sister when I wanted to go to a friend's party. So instead, I got online and played a video game."

Eden remained silent, but her hands tightened over his.

"Caron wandered off. It was hours before we found her. One of the neighbors a half mile away discovered her in the stall with one of their horses. She'd been kicked and stomped on."

"That's horrible," Eden breathed out.

"And my fault." He couldn't look at her.

She released one of his hands, and his heart sank. She was withdrawing. He knew this would happen. She blamed him just as his parents did.

Her fingers gently stroked the side of his jaw before she applied gentle pressure to turn his head toward her.

"How old were you?"

It was hard to see the compassion in her gaze. He closed his eyes. "Old enough to know better."

She cupped his cheek. "Zach, how old were you?"

"Eleven."

"You were a child left in charge of another child," she said. "This is what has kept you from wanting children of your own?"

"Yes." He grabbed her hand from his face and held it against his chest. "Don't you see? I should never be left alone with a child. What if something happened again on my watch?"

Tears crested over her lashes. He wanted to run away. But he stayed to face the censure he knew was coming.

"Oh, Zach." Her voice hitched. "You've been carrying around shame, blame and guilt all these years. This breaks my heart."

Confusion swirled within his brain. What was she saying? "But Caron got hurt because of me."

"No, Caron got hurt because she was a precocious child who wandered off looking for adventure. You were an eleven-year-old boy stuck at home with a four-year-old, when the responsibility to take care of both of you lay on your parents."

He sucked in a breath. "That's not the way my parents see it. They blamed me. And never let me forget how irresponsible I'd been. Too busy pouting and playing video games to pay attention to Caron."

"No wonder you're never excited to see them. And that's okay. Maybe one day the three of you can reconcile the unfairness of their blame." She tugged her hands from his and put them on either side of his face, forcing him to meet her eyes once again. "Zach, I want you to listen to me. You are the most responsible, compassionate, and kindest man I have ever met."

Amber's barking from around the back of the house had Zach stiffening.

The creak of a footfall on the wooden porch followed by a voice he'd hoped to never hear again, rang out, "Well, isn't this just precious."

Zach wrenched his gaze from Eden's shocked

gaze to find himself face-to-face with Jon Fielding wielding a knife in one hand and a stun gun
in the other.

Eden gasped. She couldn't believe it. How had
he gotten past the sheriff's deputy? Would this
man ever stop?

Zach stood and drew Eden to her feet but kept
her behind him. She clutched the back of his uniform shirt. Her pulse pounded in her ears. His
hand went to his holstered weapon.

"What do you think you can accomplish here,
Jon?" Zach's voice was calm, but she heard the
thread of anger beneath the surface.

"I only start what I mean to finish," Jon said. "I
know you've stashed Julie somewhere. She's not
at home or at the shelter. But I'll find her. There's
nowhere she can run, nowhere she can hide from
me. And you!" He jabbed the knife in the air.
"You told her to leave me. I read your texts and
heard your voicemail. You poisoned her against
me. She would never have had the nerve to leave
me if it weren't for you." He made a slashing motion. "I should have killed you when I had the
chance. I won't make the same mistake again."

Eden peered around Zach. "How did you find
us?"

Jon let out a laugh and stepped closer. "Everyone in town knows where the old sheriff lives."

Zach stepped back, forcing Eden to take a step

back, as well. "You'll never get to Eden without going through me."

"Then so be it. I'll take you both out." Jon lunged, leading with the knife.

Eden screamed and jumped away, allowing Zach more room to withdraw his weapons from the holster.

Jon's knife arched into the air. The stun gun arced with electricity.

Eden's breath held in her throat.

Zach let out a loud whistle as he blocked the blow from the knife with his free arm. The knife sliced through his forearm. Blood gushed from the cut.

Eden's hands curled into fists. She wanted to launch herself at Jon for hurting her husband, the man she loved.

Zach fired a shot just as Jon lunged again and the bullet missed him. From around the side of the house, Amber raced to help. The black Lab launched herself up the porch stairs, latching on to Jon's arm that held the knife. Her powerful jaws sank into his flesh, and he let out a guttural scream of pain. He dropped the stun gun but held onto the knife.

Then Piper raced to the scene, barking frantically and nipping at Jon's ankles. Jon tried to shake off both dogs, but neither canine would let go.

Eden could see there was no way Zach could shoot Jon with both dogs in the line of fire.

"Give up, Jon," Zach demanded. "You're done."

Lucy came around the corner at a run with her weapon drawn. "Drop the knife!" she shouted.

West, with Peanut at his heels, followed closely behind, his weapon also aimed at Jon.

With no other choice, Jon's hand flexed, his fingers straightening to release the knife, which clattered to the porch.

"Out." Zach gave the command and tackled Jon.

Amber released her hold on Jon and backed up a step but kept a low menacing growl going while Lucy and Zach wrestled Jon's hands behind his back and encircled his wrists with handcuffs.

The front door opened. Karl and Leslie stepped out.

Eden skirted around where Zach, dripping blood from the wound to his arm, had Jon face down on the porch and stood next to her father.

"I called 911," Karl said.

Within moments, sirens announced multiple police units arriving on the scene along with an ambulance.

"Zach's bleeding." Eden hated seeing her husband hurt.

Leslie smoothed a hand over her back. "It doesn't look life-threatening. We have to keep the faith that everything will work out."

Eden took solace in the other woman's words. Yes. She would keep the faith and hope alive that she and her husband would finally be reconciled now that she knew what drove him. She had to convince him that their love was enough to overcome his past.

Once Jon was secured in the back of Sam's Pennington County Sheriff's Department cruiser, with Sam promising he wouldn't let Jon get away again, Zach finally felt like he could breathe. The cut on his arm was superficial and didn't even require stitches. The paramedic wrapped a bandage around it and told him to change the dressing in the morning.

The deputy in the patrol car had been found tied up in his car. Jon had snuck up on him with a taser. The deputy was fine but embarrassed by letting the bad guy get the drop on him. Zach could relate. He'd been so focused on Eden that he'd allowed Jon to get too close. Now he would face jail time for his actions and Eden was finally safe.

When the chaos finally settled, Zach, West and Lucy entered the house, where Eden, Karl and Leslie had dinner ready and waiting. The aroma of grilled meat had Zach's stomach growling.

Lucy's phone rang. She glanced at the caller ID and looked at Zach and West. "It's Daniel."

Zach looked at Eden, and she waved him off. "Go talk to your boss. Then come back here. I'm hungry, emotional and I've things to say to you."

And he had things to say to her. Things that welled up into his heart wanting to burst from his throat. But he held them back so that he could join Lucy and West on the porch to talk to Daniel.

"Tell me what's happening," Daniel instructed. "I heard Jon Fielding is now back in custody."

Zach, West and Lucy filled their boss in on the evening's events.

"I'll put a call into the sheriff just to be sure Jon Fielding stays behind bars while he awaits his trial," Daniel told them. "In other news, Cheyenne managed to get a familial DNA match from the samples found on the locker of guns that you both found today, and it also matches the DNA evidence found on the weapons West and Trish discovered two months ago."

"I'm glad to hear it," West said. "We have a name?"

"Indeed. A former marine, Micah Landon, located in Fargo, North Dakota."

Lucy gasped. Her brown eyes widened. "I know Micah. He trains therapy and service dogs. He provided a dog for my daughter."

"Yes, that is the intel we have," Daniel said. "As I said, it's a familial hit, which means a blood relation to Mr. Landon."

"I don't know much about Micah's family," Lucy said.

"I'm hoping that you will use the fact that you have dealt with him before to our advantage," Daniel said. "I'd like you to head back to Fargo and interview Micah Landon."

"Of course. I'll leave in the morning," Lucy promised.

"All right, then," Daniel said. "Zach, when you're ready to jump back in, let me know."

"Copy that." Zach was grateful to his task force boss for the extra time. Time he intended to spend with his wife, if she'd have him.

The front door opened and Eden stepped into the doorway. "Everything okay here?"

"We're good." Though as Lucy and West headed inside, Zach could tell Lucy was troubled by the news about Micah Landon.

Before Eden could retreat back inside, Zach snagged her hand, loving the feel of her wedding ring on her finger, and drew her down the porch stairs and away from the house. "We didn't get to finish our conversation. Before we go in and have dinner with the others, I need to tell you something."

They stopped under the tree in the front yard. He released her hand and toyed with his own wedding band.

"Zach—"

"No, me first," he said in a rush. He felt like his chest was going to burst if he didn't let her know how much he loved her. And how much he was looking forward to being a father. "I love you, Eden Schaffer Kelcey. I have from the moment I met you. I'm not going to let fear rule my life anymore. With God and faith, I will conquer the fear. The past has no place in our future. I want to be a father to our child and a husband to you."

Eden let out a high-pitched squeal of joy and wrapped her arms around his neck. "I love you, Zach Kelcey. I'd marry you all over again. And we are going to have a baby. A shared dream. We will be the best parents that we possibly can be."

Zach dipped his head and kissed her.

When he lifted his head, he grinned at the delight on her face.

"I'm going to take tomorrow off," he told her.

"That sounds like a good idea," Eden said.

"Do you think the obstetrician could get us in so we could finally hear our baby's heartbeat?"

Her eyes widened and she grinned. "Come on, let's go call the office now and see if we can make an appointment."

"I'm sure they're closed," Zach said as he jogged alongside her toward the house.

"I can leave a message." She bounded up the stairs. Before he could make it to the top, she launched herself into his arms again. "I'm famished."

He laughed, kissed her again, and then carried her across the threshold into the house, where they joined their family and friends for dinner. And Zach couldn't wait to add more chairs to the table with their growing family.

* * * * *

*If you enjoyed Zach's story,
don't miss Lucy's story next!*

Check out Cold Case Peril
and the rest of the Dakota K-9 Unit series!

Chasing a Kidnapper
by Laura Scott, April 2025

Deadly Badlands Pursuit
by Sharee Stover, May 2025

Standing Watch
by Terri Reed, June 2025

Cold Case Peril
by Maggie K. Black, July 2025

Tracing Killer Evidence
by Jodie Bailey, August 2025

Threat of Revenge
by Jessica R. Patch, September 2025

Double Protection Duty
by Sharon Dunn, October 2025

Final Showdown
by Valerie Hansen, November 2025

Christmas K-9 Patrol
*by Lynette Eason and Lenora Worth,
December 2025*

*Available only from Love Inspired Suspense
Discover more at LoveInspired.com*

Dear Reader,

I hope you've enjoyed this third installment of the Dakota K-9 Unit continuity series. Set against the beautiful backdrop of Mount Rushmore and the Black Hills National Forest with the many parks of South Dakota, the story of Zach and Eden's journey to parenthood was filled with opposition both internally and from outside forces.

It's always a challenge to make characters sympathetic yet keep the conflict going until the dramatic resolution at the end. For Zach, he was so convinced that he didn't deserve to be a father because he was filled with shame and regret that wasn't his to bear. And Eden had let her pride and hurt feelings keep her from embracing everything her marriage could offer. But ultimately, with grace and love, they overcame the past, defeated the bad guy and have a bright future ahead of them.

I hope you will look for more of the Dakota K-9 Unit series as the task force works to bring down the illegal gun trafficking ring and discover who killed Officer Kenyon Graves.

Until we meet again, may God bless you and keep you in his care,
Terri Reed

Harlequin® Reader Service

Enjoyed your book?

Try the perfect subscription for Romance readers and get more great books like this delivered right to your door.

See why over 10+ million readers have tried Harlequin Reader Service.

Start with a Free Welcome Collection with free books and a gift—valued over $20.

Choose any series in print or ebook. See website for details and order today:

TryReaderService.com/subscriptions